From Earth I Have Arisen

A Tale of the Red Death

Matthew S. Rotundo

This story is a work of fiction. All characters, places, and incidents described in this publication are used fictitiously, or are entirely fictional.

Cover design by Jordan Malm (Instagram: @jordan.b.malm).

For exclusive content, freebies, and news from Matthew S. Rotundo, sign up for his newsletter at http://www.matthewsrotundo.com. Your email address will never be shared, and you can unsubscribe at any time.

Originally appeared in *Alembical 3*, Paper Golem, May 2014.

ISBN: 9798846157385

CONTENTS

CHAPTER ONE

FIVE MINUTES OVER PLATTSMOUTH

The hot air balloon sailed by night over the Iowa floodplain, borne on a cold northeasterly wind. The masked man in the basket, dressed all in black, gazed intently toward his target for the evening—the town of Plattsmouth, Nebraska, a mile distant, just across the Missouri River. Doubt flickered through his mind. What had at first seemed like a straightforward liberation had become much more complicated over the past several days.

"No, no," he said to himself. "None of that." He had no place for such thoughts up here. They were unworthy of Captain Dark Eagle in his trusty balloon, the *Night Wind.*

From this altitude, he could see the lights of Plattsmouth glittering. Plenty of electricity over there. Whoever was in charge clearly saw little need to ration it—and in this day and age, that was saying something. Most remaining Americans made do without power at all. Even portable generators were a luxury, and one had to scavenge for gasoline.

Momentary envy tweaked Dark Eagle. He hadn't slept in anything resembling a bed in weeks. Though he generally enjoyed the outdoors, night after night of sleeping on the cold, hard ground took its toll on his weary old joints.

Awfully cocksure, whoever was running Plattsmouth. A tinpot despot, here in America's heartland. Since the Fall, they had sprung up like noxious weeds throughout the Midwest. But whoever this one was, his time had come. Captain Dark Eagle would see to it.

Behind and above him, the steady hiss of the hot air balloon's burner, its metering valve cracked open, put out only enough flame to maintain level flight, accompanied by the omnipresent smell of propane. He could, if necessary, risk a few burns; the blast of fire would be inaudible at this altitude. The envelope's double-thick fabric, black and opaque, would mask the flame. The *Night Wind* was, for all intents and purposes in these latter days of America, the ideal stealth aircraft, perfect for reconnaissance missions like this.

To the east loomed forested bluffs that overlooked the town of Glenwood, Iowa—for all intents and purposes, a twin of Plattsmouth. Between the two towns ran the remains of a highway that crossed the river on an old bridge with rusty iron trusses.

Three days previous, he'd scouted the area, getting as close to the bridge as he dared. Concealed in the trees near the river, he'd watched for hours though his binoculars. He'd been able to make out the large sign posted on the Iowa side—a biohazard symbol over the legend *This Area QUARANTINED by Order of the United States Government.* As if to reinforce the point, armed sentries in army cammies patrolled the bridge. The sign was new, according to the reports he'd heard. So were the sentries.

At one point, an orange dump truck, its paint job faded and spattered with dried mud, had driven onto the bridge from Plattsmouth and stopped. A work crew had emerged, carrying shovels. The wind had brought a whiff of tar to him as he'd watched. The crew began working on the pavement—patching it, he supposed, preparatory to rolling over it with heavy machinery headed for Glenwood.

In better days, he gathered, the two cities had been good neighbors. But the devastation wrought by the Red Death had turned each of them into islands. And lately, Plattsmouth had closed itself off, and now threatened imminent hostilities.

Oh, what a mess he and his team had stumbled into here. Things had been simpler to the south, back home in Oklahoma. But his home was gone, as was Kathleen, and all he had ever loved. And he had a job to do.

He kept his attention focused westward. Glenwood was problematic for reasons of its own. What he knew of the place troubled him. But he would have to deal with it later.

The night was still and quiet...and cold. The last two days had brought with them a temperature swing of at least twenty degrees, presaging winter. That wasn't all bad; colder air meant the balloon required less propane to achieve buoyancy. He was down to three tanks, so any reduction in consumption could only help. Even so, Captain Dark Eagle shivered against the bracing wind. He could only fit so many layers under his black costume.

The wind direction wasn't very favorable, either. He'd had to launch from north of Glenwood, but he would likely have to land somewhere in Nebraska.

Given the situation in Plattsmouth, the bridge there was out of the question. His chase crew would have to take the trailer across the river further south, at Nebraska City, about thirty miles out of their way. That took time and fuel, neither of which they had in abundance.

Complicating matters, the wind at two thousand feet was too north-south. Dropping altitude for a more favorable wind direction would increase the chances of being spotted. He had no choice but to engage the engine.

It was his secret weapon—an electric go-kart motor mounted on a rig attached to the basket. Only fourteen horsepower, but plenty to drive a propeller and give the *Night Wind* something most hot air balloons lacked—a way to steer. Because it was electric, the motor was, like the rest of the setup, very quiet. Even so, he disliked using it. Recharging the battery could be difficult, and besides, it felt too much like cheating.

He had rigged it to pivot on its mounting, which gave him a range of about sixty degrees. It was simple enough to loosen four wing nuts, reposition the propeller, and tighten the nuts again. This he did, then started the engine. It whirred softly to life, only a little louder than the hiss of the metering valve—still quite undetectable at this range. The basket swayed a bit as he maneuvered, something he knew from the old days might have unnerved passengers unused to ballooning. He'd experienced much worse.

The engine did its work, correcting his course. He headed for the hills on the west side of the river, and the town of Plattsmouth beyond.

Captain Dark Eagle frowned at the hills. Sentries might be hidden there. Given how seriously Plattsmouth took its security, he couldn't be too careful.

He checked the instruments—altimeter, variometer, temperature gauge indicating the heat inside the envelope—and made the necessary calculations in his head. He executed another burn. It would take at least ten seconds for the balloon to respond. He'd long since become accustomed to the lag time. The balloon slowly rose. He would be over the river in less than a minute, and over the town proper seconds after that. With one gloved hand, he fingered the binoculars hanging around his neck. Well lit as the city was, he wouldn't need his night vision capabilities at all. His flight path would take him directly over the brightest area—the part of Plattsmouth he most wanted to see.

A good balloon pilot could control his altitude to within ten feet, and Captain Dark Eagle was an excellent pilot. He leveled off the *Night Wind* at 2500 feet, put his binoculars to his eyes and focused. The mask made this a bit awkward, but he'd gotten used to it with experience. Of course, he really didn't need to hide his face on an aerial reconnaissance mission; no one would see him. Indeed, no one in Plattsmouth would know of his presence. But the mask made the transition to Captain Dark Eagle palpable, enabling the proper mindset. He was a captain, and the *Night Wind* his vessel. His crew on the ground—earnest young Jaime, Jaime's father Esteban, ever-defiant Robin—didn't understand it, but they weren't called upon for understanding. If they thought Wayne Burleson an eccentric or even crazy old man, let them, so long as they obeyed.

He pushed thoughts of the ground crew out of his mind and concentrated. He was high over Plattsmouth now.

The binoculars picked out the small grid of the downtown area. Most of it was dark and quiet, actually. The well-lit area was still ahead, about three miles south-southwest of the town. As he closed in on it, he picked a long, narrow expanse of concrete that could only be a runway. A municipal airport.

Instantly, his thoughts turned to the intel Jaime, Esteban, and Robin had gathered while posing as itinerant workers in Glenwood—sightings of a jet two months ago, flying lowing in the sky, coming in for a landing somewhere to the north.

The news beggared belief. A *jet*, for the Lord's sweet sake. The *Night Wind* had been the only aircraft he'd so much as seen in years. What it meant, Captain Dark Eagle could only guess.

He cast it aside; it had no bearing at the moment. The Plattsmouth airport would be far too small to handle such traffic; Pipers and Cessnas would be more its speed. In any case, the runway boasted no aircraft of any kind. Heavy trucks stood there instead, lined up in a neat row. He counted seven in all. Numerous figures moved among them—loading or unloading, he guessed. Large crates and equipment lay about the area, unidentifiable at this range.

The wind was a little too brisk, carrying him more quickly than he would have liked. He would be over and past the airport in a matter of moments. He had to take in as much as he could and save the analysis for later.

The binoculars resolved a fence that enclosed the perimeter, topped with coils of razor wire. Patrols walked along the fence, their rifles plain to see. The place was guarded like a dad-gummed prison. He wondered if—

A bright beam flickered into life, stabbing at the sky from the north side of the airport. A searchlight.

It swung in his direction.

Captain Dark Eagle let go of his binoculars. Their weight tugged at the strap around his neck, but he was too busy gaping to care. He blinked and rubbed his eyes, thinking he had perhaps imagined it. But when he looked again, the searchlight sliced the sky and unerringly found the black envelope. A moment later, it dropped to illuminate the basket. Its brilliance bathed him.

A long wail echoed up to him—a siren. An alarm had been tripped.

Shocked and amazed, he shielded his face against the light with one hand, peering down, directly over the airport now. Even without the binoculars, he could see people scrambling on the tarmac. Some pointed at excitedly at him.

Captain Dark Eagle threw his shock aside and fired the burners again, teeth gritted, silently willing the balloon to rise. Of course, it took its time responding, lagging the burn by a full ten seconds that stretched like an age. He kept the flames roaring longer than he should, knowing he was overburning, but not caring.

Something whistled through the air past him and punched through the skirt just above his head. Something else hit the rim of the basket to his left, hard enough to make the whole assembly rock. A great chunk of wicker exploded; bits of it hit him in the face.

They were shooting at him.

Finally, the balloon began to rise, shooting skyward. He forced himself to let off the burner before the temperature inside the envelope got hot enough to start the fabric on fire.

He was south of the airport. They'd stopped firing at him; the balloon was out of range. But the searchlight still tracked him. He grabbed the binoculars and looked back. People were scrambling into vehicles—smaller trucks than the ones lined up on the runway, no doubt with off-road capabilities.

Despite the cold air, sweat ran down his face, stinging his eyes. He was at three thousand feet and still climbing. But sooner or later, he would have to land...and with that searchlight on him, they would see where he went down. They'd reach him long before his chase crew could.

He glanced over his instruments. The wind at this altitude blew due south. And—

His gaze lighted on the engine. He lunged for it, making the basket bob. One hand gripped a handle while the other loosened the first of the four wing nuts. When the basket had settled again, he released the handle and went to work on the other three. The fourth slipped from his grasp and fell. He reached for it and missed; it disappeared into the night.

The basket tipped alarmingly with the shift in weight. He would have tumbled out had he not leaned hard in the opposite direction. The basket stabilized, but the engine slid off kilter. He grabbed for it and repositioned the propeller, even as the balloon rocked. He ignored it, focused only on tightening down the wing nuts before he lost another one.

Overhead, the envelope flapped in the wind—a signal that the balloon was changing direction. The sound eased some of his tension; his fingers worked more smoothly, locking the engine into position once again. He found himself perversely grateful for the illumination the searchlight provided.

He looked northward. The *Night Wind* was about a mile past Plattsmouth. On the ground, a line of headlights proceeded from the airport, all headed south.

He glanced at his compass, grabbed his radio. "*Night Wind* to ground, copy?"

Jaime's voice came back immediately: "We copy, *Night Wind.* What—"

"I've been spotted. They're tracking me right now. I'm coming across—"

A burst of static flared. A moment later, Robin said, "*What* did you say?"

Anger surged in Captain Dark Eagle. Through gritted teeth, he said, "Robin, give the radio back to Jaime and concentrate on driving."

"Wayne, are you telling us—"

"*Now!*" Spittle flew from his lips. He wiped it off the radio with a sleeve.

Jaime came back on: "Ah, could you repeat that, *Night Wind*?"

"You heard me the first time: I've been spotted. I'm blown. And they're coming after me. Keep quiet and listen. We have to abort our original plan. I'm coming back across the river. I'm a little over a mile south of Plattsmouth, bearing"—he checked his compass—"one-five-six. You need to find me a place to land. Now. Where are you?"

"Ah—" Some crackling came over the speaker, as of paper rustling. "Southbound on I-29. Just coming up on Glenwood."

"Good. Are there any other vehicles in sight?"

A pause. Then, "No. None."

"All right. Keep your—"

"Holy sh—I mean, holy smokes! We can see the spotlight! We see you, *Night Wind*!"

"Not for long, if I can help it. Once I get over the river, I'm dropping altitude. The hills will hide me then. And you need to have a place for me to land."

"Copy, *Night Wind.* I—hold on a minute." A confused babble of voices, too faint for Dark Eagle to make out. Then Jaime said, "Robin says to just come down by the Interstate. It's clear—no power lines, no trees."

"You're sure about the power lines?"

"Robin says she's sure. She says she remembers scouting the area on the way up from Missouri."

Captain Dark Eagle closed his eyes for a moment and gave silent thanks for Robin.

He opened his eyes, looking down. The dark bulk of the hills along the west side of the river rose below him. "All right, fine. Keep your headlights on, so I can see you."

"Copy, *Night Wind*."

"And be ready to move *fast*. We'll have to set a new speed record for packing up. Understand?"

Another voice in the background—Robin's, he thought. Jaime said. "Ah—if you're being chased, shouldn't we ditch the balloon?"

"Under no circumstances."

"But—"

"No discussion. You heard me. Just be ready. I'll be coming down hard, copy?"

"Ah…copy, *Night Wind*."

The doubt was evident in Jaime's voice, and Robin would only feed it. But Jaime had sense enough to follow orders, even if he didn't like them.

Captain Dark Eagle was not in the habit of explaining himself to subordinates, especially in crisis situations. But by his reckoning, those chasing him from Plattsmouth had made a key tactical mistake: they'd set out after him on a north-south highway on the Nebraska side of the river. They'd mistakenly assumed he wouldn't be able to get back to Iowa. They were already well south of the bridge. By the time they figured out where he was going, they would have to double back north just to get across—which would delay them. Enough, Captain Dark Eagle hoped, for him and his team to pack up the balloon and make their getaway.

He had a hunch that his pursuers would lose interest once they lost sight of him. For the present, they seemed more concerned with maintaining their borders than with launching some ill-considered foray into Iowa to find a mysterious black balloon.

Satisfied with his trajectory, he pulled the venting line. The hateful searchlight tracked him unerringly; whoever operated it was skilled.

The balloon began to descend. Captain Dark Eagle looked northward, smiled, and waved, though he knew he couldn't be seen. "Farewell, my friends. I'll be back."

He came down gratifyingly fast. The variometer showed a descent rate of 500 feet per minute. The dark hills rose, as if growing before his eyes. Even so, it took a full two minutes before the balloon finally sank behind their cover, blocking the searchlight.

His smile faded. All business, he faced southeast, the direction of travel. Landmarks were difficult to make out, but as near as he could tell, he had crossed the river.

Once again invisible, he had to fight the urge to relax. For all he knew, the entire town of Plattsmouth was mobilizing to come after him—though he tended to doubt it. Even so, better to assume the worst, given the situation.

As he flew, he pondered what he'd seen and what had happened. It was the first time he'd been sighted on a reconnaissance flight. He mentally replayed the mission, analyzing his burns and maneuvers for any mistakes he'd made, any slips that might have tipped his hand. He couldn't think of any. If anything, he'd been extra cautious with his approach—and to no avail.

Behind him, the engine purred. He reached back and patted its housing. It had likely saved his life tonight. Another narrow escape, the latest in a series of them.

Maybe he *was* crazy—an insanity that threatened not only him, but everyone he came in contact with.

He cut off that line of thinking before it could go any further. Whatever the state of his mental health, he had chosen his path. He couldn't undo any of what he'd done, even if he wanted to.

Light in his peripheral vision startled him. He turned in that direction. It came from the ground north of his position—a set of headlights, maybe a mile distant. He got on the two-way again: "*Night Wind* to ground. I'm over the river and looking north. Flash your lights twice."

"Copy, *Night Wind*," Jaime said.

Obligingly, the headlights blinked off and on, off and on. He had expected as much—the Red Death had all but killed vehicular traffic, too—but he hadn't come this far by being careless.

"All right, I see you," he said. "Are we still clear?"

"Roger that, *Night Wind*."

With one hand on the venting line, he groped along his belt line until he found the flashlight he'd clipped there. He pointed it toward the ground, flicked it on. "Can you see me, ground?"

"Ah, check. Roger, *Night Wind*."

"I'm landing. Altitude"—he checked his instruments—"six hundred feet."

As he'd promised, he came down like a stone. For the last fifty feet, he pulled the red line instead of the venting line—something one normally did after landing, as it started deflating the balloon. Doing so in flight was reserved only for emergencies.

He expected that it would make the landing that much harder, and he was not disappointed. The basket hit the ground with bone jarring force and promptly fell over. Captain Dark Eagle would have tumbled out but for his grip on one of the handles. The wind dragged the balloon another fifteen or twenty feet before friction finally brought it to a stop. He got a face full of dirt and weeds for his trouble, but nothing worse than that.

Less than a minute later, Robin, Jaime, and Esteban were there, righting the basket and putting their weight on it. Wayne Burleson took off the mask, shut off the burners and the engine, and clambered out. Tall roadside weeds tugged at his pants.

Upon successful landing, SOP was to link hands in a circle, while Wayne led them in a brief prayer of thanks. Circumstances dictated otherwise this time. Wayne contented himself with muttering a few words his flight instructor had said upon the conclusion of Wayne's first solo flight, so many years ago: "From Earth I have arisen. To Earth I have returned."

The others nodded in understanding. They set to work immediately, speaking only when necessary, all business.

Robin was a tiny thing, barely five feet and so thin he often feared for her health. Her tattered ball cap covered her close-cropped hair. She dressed in shapeless clothing than hung off her. And homosexual, too. She had been very upfront about that, from the moment they had met. Wayne didn't approve, of course, for all that mattered. Twenty-five, or so she claimed, though she looked like a teenager—even younger than Jaime, who was eighteen.

Jaime was the image of his father twenty years younger. Both had the same jet-black hair, the same pinched features, the same compact but broad-shouldered frames. Esteban had worked in a packinghouse before the Red Death, probably illegally. His son spoke English much better, and often translated for his father. A lesbian and an illegal immigrant and that man's son—that was his team. Such a far cry from the life he'd had, the life with his dear Kathleen. The Lord worked in mysterious ways, indeed.

The envelope sagged and lay on the ground, though it still bulged with the remaining hot air. At the top of the envelope, Esteban stood with the crown ring positioned in the small of his back, keeping the load cables taut, expediting deflation. Jaime bustled at the basket, flushing the propane lines. From the trailer, Robin retrieved the straps, the envelope bag, and the squeeze bar. Wayne forced himself to focus on the task at hand, and to put away thoughts of anyone coming after them. They were all armed and capable of defending themselves, should the worst happen. Even so, he silently prayed that bloodshed wouldn't be necessary tonight. He had too much to think over.

They'd practiced this drill so many times as a team that not even the darkness impeded them. Robin ran the squeeze bar down the length of the envelope, forcing out the last of the heated air, while Wayne, Jaime, and Esteban followed, bundling the envelope with straps as they went. They stuffed the envelope in its bag, not bothering to ensure it was properly folded. The burner assembly and the engine mount were tossed into the basket for the time being without being properly broken down. The team loaded everything into their rickety trailer—black, like the *Night Wind.* By his best estimate—his watch batteries had died some six months ago, and he hadn't been able to scavenge replacement for them—they finished the job in maybe twenty minutes from touchdown. And still the surrounding countryside remained dark and undisturbed by headlights or the rumble of engines.

They got into the truck and raced south. Without being told, Robin turned east at the earliest opportunity, onto a rough dirt track that jostled them hard enough to make Wayne grateful for his seat belt. Without it, he would have bumped his head repeatedly on the roof of the cab.

Despite the cold, all of them dripped perspiration. Wayne wiped at his forehead. "That was good work, team. I'm proud of you."

They nodded and gave grim smiles—all except Robin, who focused on driving.

Impressive as the job had been, though, he knew it hadn't been good enough. As he'd suspected, the Plattsmouth people hadn't come across the river. If they had, they would have almost certainly caught up to the *Night Wind* and its crew. Backtracking to the bridge would have taken them out of their way, but not *that* far. At best, Wayne's maneuver had bought him and his crew ten or fifteen minutes, tops.

The others probably knew it, too.

Well, he'd never promised them it would be easy—or safe.

Robin finally broke the silence: "What the *fuck* happened?"

"Watch your language, young lady." He told them what had happened, omitting nothing. It didn't take long.

When he finished, he checked their reactions. Jaime's eyes were wide, his mouth slightly agape. Next to him in the back seat, Esteban sat as expressionless as always. Wayne couldn't tell if that was just the man's demeanor, or if he simply didn't understand much English.

Robin, on the other hand—

"Jesus Christ, Wayne. How could you let this happen?"

"You know I feel about blasphemy, Robin."

She slammed a fist into the cracked dashboard. "This is fucked. Now we have *another* town hunting us."

Jaime spoke from the back seat: "How could they have sighted you? The *Night Wind* should have been invisible."

"It was. It is."

"Maybe they knew you were coming," Robin said. "Maybe this Serena Katz woman in Glenwood set you up."

The thought had occurred to Wayne, but he discounted it immediately. Robin openly distrusted Serena Katz, and not without reason. Even so—"If she wanted to set us up, she went to an awful lot of trouble. There had to be easier ways."

Robin clenched the steering wheel, still fuming. Wayne couldn't blame her. The debacle at Independence still weighed on her, on all of them.

Jaime said, "So now what?"

Wayne stared into the surrounding darkness. "Now we go back to Glenwood and find out what's really going on here."

CHAPTER TWO

AMERICA IS DEAD

The *Night Wind* and her captain flew again two nights later, destined for a rendezvous with Serena Katz, the woman in the castle.

She stood alone in the large field south of Glenwood—perhaps five foot nine, sturdily built, short hair, dark but heavily salted gray. She might have been his age. She kept a respectful distance as the *Night Wind* descended, standing ten feet back, arms crossed. When he touched down—much more gently than the previous landing—she said, "Captain. You honor us again."

Serena was the reason they'd come to Glenwood in the first place. They had fled Independence northward on Interstate 29, the best available road. Hard winters and lack of maintenance had taken their toll, of course, but the interstate highways remained mostly passable—for the time being. Shortly after crossing the Missouri-Iowa border, they had found the first sign by the side of the road—neatly hand-painted, secured in the ground on two posts. It read, *CAPTAIN DARK EAGLE, GLENWOOD NEEDS YOU!* Below that, in smaller print: *Fields south of Highway 34. We'll be waiting, watching, and praying.*

The sign had given them all a turn. For his part, Wayne Burleson felt equal parts elation and consternation. Word of the liberations had spread. Nowata, Oklahoma. Liberal, Kansas. Maybe even Independence, Missouri, God help them. The Internet was dead, but ham radio was alive and well.

On the other hand, no one had ever before *summoned* Captain Dark Eagle.

They had come across two more such signs before Wayne finally decided to officially make for Glenwood.

It already seemed like an age ago. "Save it, Colonel," Captain Dark Eagle said. He allowed just enough flame to keep the envelope inflated. She *was* a colonel, or so she had claimed at their first meeting. USAF, retired. She'd been stationed at Offutt Air Force Base—formerly SAC Headquarters—just outside of Omaha, about twenty miles to the north. "You have some explaining to do. I nearly got shot down on your account."

Her smiled faded. "Yes, so I saw. One of my sentries spotted the searchlight and alerted me. A lot of other people saw it, too. By the next morning, everyone in town was talking about your black balloon."

So they all knew he was here. That posed some potential security risks. Spilt milk, at this point. But at least none of them knew of his team, nor did they know that he had also flown reconnaissance over Glenwood even before that first rendezvous.

It was part of the same mission that had sent Robin, Jaime, and Esteban into the town to gather what intel they could. Glenwood was much more receptive to itinerant workers than places like Plattsmouth, rewarding a few days' hard work with some provisions. And while his team had toiled incognito by day, he had by night overflown Glenwood. From the air, the town was nothing remarkable. With his night vision binoculars, he'd spotted a few civilian sentries keeping watch on the roads leading into town—the usual stuff. Simple prudence in the age after the Red Death.

But nestled in the bluffs overlooking the city was the castle.

From the air, it had resembled nothing else. Well lit, it glittered like a jewel among the surrounding trees. That would take a heavy toll on the generators that powered it. Expansive grounds, brick structures, a central tower of stone, all engirthed by—there could be no mistaking it—a moat. Only one road snaked into the hills to its front gate.

Well lit, and also well guarded. With the aid of his binoculars, he had noted two fortified sentry positions on either side of the gate, and at least three armed foot patrols walking the perimeter. Whoever lived in that castle had gone to some trouble to advertise how much muscle they had at their disposal—clearly unafraid of the bands of marauders roving though the countryside since the Fall.

It had been enough to convince Captain Dark Eagle that some strongman had set up shop there, ruling Glenwood with an iron fist.

He'd come to that first meeting expecting to find some poor denizens of Glenwood, speaking in fearful whispers of the man in the castle. But as it happened, Serena *was* the man in the castle.

The mayor of Glenwood had succumbed to the Red Death. So had the deputy mayor, the sheriff, and the entire city council. The good citizens had appointed her to take their place. *Someone had to take charge, get us organized,* she had said. As for the castle, it had formerly been a resort hotel. Serena had converted it to a headquarters.

The real problem, Captain, she'd said, *is over the river. On the other side is a town called Plattsmouth. They've become heavily armed and quite belligerent. They've told us that they're gearing up for a move across the bridge, coming for us. We know too little of their capabilities. I was hoping you could do some recon for us. We need your help, Captain.*

Those words had set him on the path that led to this second meeting.

Arranging it had required some creativity. At Dark Eagle's orders, Jaime had snuck back into town—a relatively easy task for one person against volunteer sentries—and left a folded note prominently addressed *Lt. Colonel Serena Katz—Personal and Confidential* at the community center. The note gave the time, date, and location, and was signed only with a simple drawing of a balloon.

"You've stirred up quite a hornet's nest here, Captain," Serena said.

"*You* stirred up the hornet's nest. But you haven't told me everything."

She opened her hands in a *what-can-I-do?* gesture. "I don't know much more than you do at this point. In fact, your intel has to be better than mine."

"How could Plattsmouth have known I was coming?"

"They didn't. It's impossible." She shook her head emphatically. "I'm the only one from Glenwood who knew of our last meeting. I assure you, I told no one."

"They detected me, then."

"Yes."

"Which means they have some way to track aircraft in the dark. Radar, I'm guessing, and personnel capable of operating it. Add to that at least one large searchlight and several large trucks, and we're talking about capabilities that would seem to be beyond the resources of a small town. Even before the Red Death, civil defense budgets were never that large."

Serena glanced away. "Yes."

The envelope bobbed and swayed with the breeze. He had the enough hot air in there to keep it just below the balance point. A sudden gust might carry him a few feet, or even knock over the balloon. The motion reminded him he needed to keep this short.

"Colonel, I know about that airplane your people saw."

"What of it?"

"Don't play stupid with me; you don't do it very well. It landed north of town. My guess is at Offutt Air Force Base—your old outfit."

"Yes, probably."

"So the United States military has sent a plane to Offutt—a big one. That means a lot of personnel and equipment. A few months later, the town across the river starts exhibiting military-grade gear and tactics."

Captain Dark Eagle had no doubt those uniformed sentries were professional soldiers. In another life, he'd been a veteran of the Seventy-fifth Ranger Regiment, Second Battalion—with a Second Battalion tattoo on his right shoulder to prove it—and he had a nose for his own. "Whatever that plane's mission here," he said, "it involves more than just securing an Air Force base. They're spreading out, expanding."

Serena crossed her arms. "We don't know who flew that plane in. And yes, they're expanding. They've taken Plattsmouth, and they say Glenwood is next."

He pointed northward. "You think some petty local warlord commandeered a military aircraft and flew it in here?"

"Again, I don't know, and I don't care. My first and only priority is the safety of Glenwood. That's where my loyalty lies."

"They've posted signs warning that Plattsmouth has been quarantined."

She shook her head. "Yes, I know. I'm the one who told you that. So what?"

"So why, after all these years of the Red Death, does the city of Plattsmouth suddenly quarantine itself? Why do they care now?"

The Red Death wasn't gone, of course. It still lurked in the remains of the larger cities, and in numerous deserted small towns across the country. But those with effective quarantine procedures had escaped with their lives, if nothing else. So many years later, there was little need for such measures. With the widespread collapse of social order and the transportation infrastructure, the disease could no longer travel freely. One needed only to avoid the hotspots.

The greater danger, these days, came from those seeking to fill the power vacuum.

Serena dismissed Dark Eagle's concerns with a swipe of one hand. "Maybe they've had an outbreak."

"That's what I thought at first, too. But if that were the case, why would they let their sentries walk around in the open air without any protection? If the area is quarantined, why aren't they wearing full hazmat gear?"

"Careless, maybe."

"Oh, I doubt that. I have a better idea." He took a breath and spoke the words he had hardly dared allowed himself to think: "They've developed a vaccine for the Red Death, haven't they? They delivered it to Offutt, and now they're spreading it to the surrounding locales. When they got to Plattsmouth, they closed the borders, using quarantine as a cover story, to prevent any outbreaks before they could get everyone in town vaccinated."

She looked away.

It was all the confirmation he needed. "They told you as much, didn't they? And now they want to vaccinate Glenwood."

She sneered. "Under the circumstances, they would have said anything."

His heart raced as he considered the implications. After all these years, after all the dark things he had seen and done, finally, his faith had been vindicated. He shook his head with slow disbelief. "And you want to resist them? Are you insane? You want to stop them from saving everyone in Glenwood?"

"I have no reason to trust them. Even if they have a vaccine, we don't need it. We're doing just fine on our own, thank you. We certainly don't need to allow a bunch of strangers with weapons to just waltz in here and do whatever they please." She began circling the basket, slowly, still keeping her distance. "I had hoped that you of all people would understand that, Captain."

He turned as she walked, not presenting his back to her, not even for a moment. "I understand that the United States of America never fell. We might have stumbled, even lost our way, but I always knew we would be back. And now it's starting to happen. This is the first step. There are probably planes flying out all over the country, even as we speak. We can finally restore the order."

She hung her head as if weary. "Oh, Captain, come on. After all your travels, all those liberations, after everything you've seen, you still haven't figured it out?" She flapped a hand in his direction. "I mean, I always assumed that this get-up, this act of yours, was something to impress the mooks. I never thought for one moment that you took any of it seriously—that you believed this nonsense."

Captain Dark Eagle straightened and raised his chin. "All those liberations—nonsense? That airplane—is that nonsense, too? Rebuilding America—nonsense?"

She stopped circling. In a low voice, she said, "My son died."

"You can't—beg pardon?"

She raised her voice a little. "He died. Twenty-one years old. And that isn't nonsense; it's the hard truth. Would you like to know it happened? It wasn't the Red Death."

Dark Eagle held his silence but feared he could guess what she would say.

"When the President made his final televised address—remember it? When he declared martial law?"

He remembered. He still had trouble thinking of the man as the last acting President of the United States. Just a few days previous, he had been Secretary of Agriculture. But the Red Death had taken everyone else ahead of him in the line of succession.

And though he had never used the words *martial law* in that address, the intent had been clear to anyone watching.

"My son joined the protest marchers in Des Moines," Serena said. "They gunned him down, along with a few thousand others.

One of his college friends called me with the news. It was the last cell phone call I ever received."

Dark Eagle held his gaze steady on her, but her words weighed on his soul. He had seen footage of similar outrages.

"Captain, you asked me if I thought some petty warlord had flown that plane in. I don't. I believe those men are exactly who they say they are. And that's I won't let them into Glenwood." She pointed toward the west. "Even if they're acting under orders, I have no confidence in the politicians who gave those orders. They're the kind of people who let this happen. They betrayed all of us. They spent so much of their time spending money they didn't have, fighting wars they didn't need to fight, and clinging to their failed ideologies, that when the Red Death hit, when we as a nation most needed vision and leadership, we got platitudes and paralysis. And when that didn't work, they resorted to martial law and mass slaughter." She spat. "No more, Captain. I'm not letting them put Glenwood under their thumb, ever again. America is dead. I do not share your necrophilia for the United States."

The envelope swayed again in the breeze. Captain Dark Eagle felt it tugging at the basket. An urge for the buoyancy of flight stole over him.

"Captain," she said, "see reason. You can't go back to the way it was, but you can still do some good. You *have* done some good. You're brave and honorable; anyone can see that. And we need to know Plattsmouth's capabilities. Will you help us?"

They stared at each other across the weed-choked field. A great sadness took hold of Captain Dark Eagle. In another life, under other circumstances, this would have been a woman to stand by his side. He might have been honored to serve under her command. But her path had diverged from his long ago. "I'm sorry for the loss of your son, Colonel, but the people who made those decisions are dead. If that isn't justice, I don't know what is. Now we finally have a chance at a new start, and you've chosen to nurse your anger, to give in to despair. You won't give America another chance. I can't do that. I'll pray for you."

He fired the burners full blast; the flames roared into the envelope. The *Night Wind* rose, and the breeze carried him away from her. She only stood there as he departed. She made no move toward the balloon, uttered no protestations. Naturally not. Her pride wouldn't allow it.

She was lost to the darkness. He turned faced forward, borne on a light westerly breeze. He pulled out his radio. "*Night Wind* to ground, copy?"

"Right here, Captain," Jaime said.

"Where's *here*?"

"Ah, let me check the map…it says County Highway H40."

A few miles south of him, if memory served.

"I'm airborne, eastbound from the rendezvous point. I need to set down as soon as possible. Get out there and scout me a location."

"Roger that. We'll—"

He cut off. Captain Dark Eagle frowned at the radio. "Ground, you copy? Ground?"

Strange sounds came from the speaker—angry shouts, voices he didn't recognize, repeated pops that might have been gunshots.

"Ground! Come in! Ground! What—"

A scream. Robin, unmistakably.

Then, smooth silence.

"Ground! Status report! That's an order! Ground!"

He looked over the radio to make sure he hadn't accidentally switched it off. The green power indicator was still lit. The problem had to be with Jaime's unit.

He stared into the night, thinking furiously. From here, he was powerless to help his crew—and they seemed powerless to help him. His first order of business had to be landing safely, without their assistance. Then he would see about—

The radio crackled in his hand. "Captain Dark Eagle, do you read?"

The voice was a woman's, familiar.

"Captain? I know you can hear me."

He recognized her then. It had only taken longer because hers was the last voice he would have expected coming over his radio—Serena Katz.

Dark thoughts and dread swirled through his mind. He licked his lips, spoke into the radio: "This is Captain Dark Eagle."

"I tried reasoning with you, Captain. I wish you would have listened. It would have been so much easier for everyone involved. I deeply regret that it's come to this."

"What have you done?" He feared he already knew.

"Did you really think that I wouldn't know about strangers coming into my town? It's not like we get a lot of visitors these days. So when three new faces arrive looking for work, naturally I was more than a little curious. Simple prudence."

"What have you done, Colonel?"

"I had my people hide a bird dog tracking collar in those provisions we supplied you with. In the old days, they were easy enough to find in your local sporting goods store. Popular with hunters, you understand. These collars have an effective range of about twenty miles."

Captain Dark Eagle closed his eyes for a moment, cursing himself for a fool. Inspecting the goods had never even occurred to him.

"We've known exactly where your team's been for the last several days. I had my people standing by outside your camp while you and I talked, just in case things didn't work out."

"What have you—"

"We have your young friend…Jaime, I believe his name is? He's quite safe, as is the rest of your team—but I'm afraid we had to shoot out the tires on your truck to prevent pursuit."

Captain Dark Eagle banged a fist against the side of the basket.

Serena went on, her voice smooth, even a little smug: "We don't want Jaime—or anyone else—hurt. But I need your cooperation, Captain, and I intend to get it."

His grip on the radio tightened, making his hand hurt. "What do you want?"

"For starters, your recon report on Plattsmouth. I want to know everything you saw, what we'll be up against. And I'll want the *Night Wind*, too—just in case. Waste not, want not."

He looked around, searching the dark land below for any sign of movement, hoping he might find the vehicle Serena's people had used to abduct Jaime. If they were smart, they would be running without headlights. Even if he managed to catch a glimpse of them, he could hardly give chase, not with limited maneuverability and low fuel. Speaking of which—

He glanced at the propane tank's gauge. It registered fifteen percent. The bottom ten percent of the tank was useless, lacking enough pressure to push out the gas. Which meant he had only another few minutes of flight time.

"Captain?" Serena said. "Are you still reading me?"

He pulled his attention away from the gauge. "How do I know you actually have him? How do I know he's safe?"

That she knew which channel he was using was evidence enough that she had at least gotten hold of Jaime's radio. He was stalling; he could think of nothing else to do.

Amusement showed in her voice: "My people are listening to this conversation. They'll put your young friend on."

A moment of silence. Then, Jaime said, "I'm sorry, Captain. They came out of nowhere. Took us completely by surprise."

The sound of Jaime's voice made it all seem more real. Until that moment, shock had made it feel like some kind of weird dream. "Are you hurt?"

"I took a couple of hits to the body. I think I broke one guy's nose, though."

Captain Dark Eagle smiled grimly. "Good work."

"Don't give in to them. Whatever they're asking for ransom, don't—"

A racket came over the radio—someone wresting it away from Jaime, probably. Then Serena spoke again: "It would be unwise for you to heed your friend's advice. Very unwise."

"And what if I did? What would you do to him?"

"These are hard times, Captain. Don't make them any harder."

"Give it up, Serena. You can't win this. If you kill him, you'll have no hold over me—and no chance of ever gaining my cooperation. And are you really willing to become what you've beheld in order to get your way? I don't think you are." He believed it, too. She wouldn't dare. Or would she?

"You know what I think, Captain? I think all your bluff and bluster is just that. I think beneath that cornball costume, there is a practical man. And I *know* you don't have so many friends that you can afford to throw one away."

His lips skinned back over his teeth. "Here's one thing you *don't* know about me, Serena: I don't negotiate with terrorists."

He snapped off the radio without waiting for a reply. He needed to concentrate on landing, anyway.

The last of the shock wore away, leaving cold anger in its wake. *America is dead*, Serena Katz had said. Well, she would discover to her sorrow just how wrong she was. He would personally see to it.

CHAPTER THREE

DELUSIONS OF GRANDEUR

With only the light of a sliver of moon to guide him, Captain Dark Eagle set down near a copse of tall trees. In the darkness, though, he didn't realize how hilly the area was—until he landed. The basket hit the ground at a bad angle and tumbled. The impact threw him out; he maintained his grip on a handle by force of will, though it felt for one terrifying moment that the balloon would rip his arm from its socket.

By the time the *Night Wind* finally came to a rest, his head, midsection, and legs ached from numerous thumps and contusions. His mask, knocked askew, partially obstructed his vision. He considered himself fortunate not to have broken anything.

He picked himself up from the ground and brushed himself off. He removed his mask and took stock of the situation.

Serena's people had Jaime's radio, which gave Wayne no way of communicating with Robin and Esteban. If Serena could be believed, the truck had lost at least two tires, and there was only one spare. Robin and Esteban could not afford to abandon the trailer and all its supplies. They were going nowhere. That left Wayne with a painful alternative: he would have to ditch the balloon and go to them.

He looked over the *Night Wind*, lying on its side like a wounded animal. He could not simply leave it in the open like this. It had to be secured—as well as it could be, given the circumstances.

His instincts tugged at him, reminding him that Jaime had been kidnapped. He disengaged his roiling emotions, a handy trick he'd learned during his ranger days. He wasn't going to help Jaime by rushing off pell-mell into the darkness. Serena had gotten the better of him—for the moment—and nothing could be done about it tonight. No need to compound a bad situation by making emotional judgments.

Deflating the envelope alone drained him. Each passing minute weighed on him like a stone. Forcing himself to focus on the task at hand took real energy. Oh, but that woman had done a number on him.

For the *Night Wind*, the best he could do was roll up the envelope into a rough ball, cables still attached, and stuff as much as would fit into the basket. The rest of it overflowed the top like a mushroom. He took off the burner assembly and the motor mounting and stowed them among the nearby trees. He also disconnected the nearly empty propane tank and concealed it in some underbrush. The basket and envelope he could only drag downhill and wrangle into what he hoped was an inconspicuous spot under the canopy of a large weeping willow.

The entire operation took him at least an hour, probably more, and left him exhausted, thirsty, and aching. By daylight, he was sure, the balloon would be easy enough to find—but only if someone were looking for it. No roads ran near this hill, so any discovery would be on foot. The *Night Wind* should be safe for at least a few days, possibly several weeks. Or so Wayne told himself.

And besides, he had no choice. Plenty of pilots had been forced to ditch their balloons. He'd heard stories of emergency landings in mountainous country inaccessible except by helicopter. The cost of retrieving a balloon from such areas would have been more than the balloon itself was worth, so most pilots simply abandoned them.

This, by comparison, should be easy. He wasn't abandoning the *Night Wind*. He silently vowed he would be back for it as soon as he could.

He turned away from the weeping willow. County Road H40, Jaime had said. If Wayne headed due south, he should run across it. He swigged the last of the bottled water he'd brought with him on this flight and started walking. A familiar pang of loss and sadness stabbed at his guts, hard enough to rock him on his feet. He staggered but kept on, knowing that if he stopped, paralysis would overtake him. It wasn't the first time he'd walked away.

"I'll be back," he whispered. "From Earth I have arisen. To Earth I have returned."

No, not the first time. He hadn't been at Katheen's side when she'd died. She wouldn't allow it.

Uneven ground made for slow going in the darkness. As he trudged along, the memory sprang unbidden to his mind, filled his thoughts.

"You can't…stay here," she had said between raspy breaths. "You'll get it, too."

"No, I'll be fine. You don't worry about me."

He had worked to keep his voice cheerful. The surroundings had made it difficult. The hospital in Nowata was tiny and overrun. The overhead fluorescents flickered every few minutes as the overworked generators struggled to keep pace with the demand.

They'd squeezed Kathleen into a cot in the corner of the basement, behind a set of washing machines. An IV line attached to her arm kept her hydrated, but the hospital had no other medical equipment to spare. Six other cots had been crammed into the basement, all occupied by patients in the throes of the Red Death. Wayne thought the one nearest the door may have expired recently; the wasted body lay motionless on its cot, the skin gone gray where it hadn't been mottled by the telltale rash.

The smell in the place was terrible—a sickening mixture of urine, feces, and rot. The surgical mask he wore—provided for him when he'd brought Kathleen in two days previous—did nothing to screen it out.

Still, the corner behind the washing machines, though cramped, afforded them a modicum of privacy. At least Kathleen wouldn't have to see the other victims. And the dim lighting made her own rashes seem somehow less severe.

By that time, they had already lost all their children and grandchildren. Melinda had been the last to go, their eldest daughter. Wayne and Kathleen had gone out to Melinda's farm to tend her as best they could. Kathleen had come home with a fever. Wayne had not.

He had been fool enough to believe that their isolated life on an acreage in northern Oklahoma had been enough to keep them from getting sick. Indeed, he had watched the news reports of cities becoming burning charnel houses and had given thanks to God that he and Kathleen had been spared.

Then had come the news that Robert and his entire family in Wichita had succumbed in a matter of days. Then Deborah and the twins, in Dallas. Then Melinda.

And finally, at the end, with civilization collapsing around them, with reports of widespread riots and looting, Kathleen had gotten sick.

It had been Wayne's idea to take her to the nearest hospital, in Nowata, thirty miles away. His one hope was that they could keep her alive long enough for the CDC to find a cure—if there even *was* a CDC anymore.

He had enough gas in the truck to get her to Nowata. If that hadn't worked, he would have figured something else out. By God, he would have taken her by air if he had to. In the years since his retirement from the Army, he'd taken up hot air ballooning, and become a skilled pilot. He occasionally supplemented their income by selling rides.

They'd arrived in Nowata to find the tiny hospital in chaos. As near as Wayne could tell, only one doctor and three nurses remained to tend the dying—which primarily consisted of saline solutions to stave off dehydration and aspirin to tamp down the fever. Both were by then in short supply. Kathleen's last aspirin had come twelve hours ago, and her saline bag was nearly empty.

"You haven't slept in days," she said.

"Neither have you. Don't worry about me, heart."

She slowly shook her head. "You're all…I have left…to worry about."

He patted her hand. "You worry about resting."

"I'll have plenty of rest…soon enough."

"Don't talk like that."

"I'll talk how I like." She drew a rattling breath. "I don't have time to argue, Wayne Burleson. You need to go home. Before they get here."

They were the vicious marauders reported via ham radio to be heading up Highway 169 from Oologah. Nowata still had some semblance of social order, and so had drawn a lot of survivors. Prudent rationing had saved a significant portion of the last harvest. What they didn't have, so far as Wayne could tell, was a stockpile of weapons and people trained in their use.

The hospital and grounds were shut off from the rest of the town by stout barricades. Behind them, the survivors hid, girding themselves to protect what little they still had.

The remaining hospital staff had refused to abandon their posts, God bless them.

Wayne, having been in such close proximity to the Red Death, would not be allowed behind the barricades. He bore the denizens of Nowata no ill will over the matter; he would have done the same, had the situation been reversed. That left him with only two options—to remain in the hospital, or to return to the acreage.

"You'll be safe there," Kathleen said.

Wayne shook his head. "The only way I leave here is if you're with me. I won't be budged. You know me better than that." He gave her a soft smile, stroked her thinning white hair.

Her face remained grim. "Oh, I know you, all right. Better than you think." She grimaced and spasmed, clutching her midsection.

He glanced around, searching in vain for one of the nurses. He slipped an arm under her head. "Do you need to vomit? Let me help you up. I'll—"

"No." She grimaced again, then relaxed. "No, it'll pass. I need you…to listen."

Her tone of voice brooked no dissent. He gently removed his arm, letting her settle back on the pillow. "I'm listening, heart."

She fixed her gaze on him; he reciprocated. He looked into her dear face. Sallow and sunken though her features had become, he still knew every line, still saw the girl he had married over fifty years ago, neither one dreaming then that it would eventually come to this.

"I know you," she said. "You want to follow me…to the grave."

"Don't talk like—"

"You think there's nothing left for you. Nothing left to live for. You stay, and they kill you when you get here. That's…what you want."

"Nonsense." Her words bit, but he would not allow his pain to show.

"Don't backtalk me. Your mother raised you better."

He held his tongue. She was right; she knew him all too well.

"You heed me, Wayne Burleson: you're not allowed to die. Not here. Not yet."

On a nearby cot, someone moaned and called out for his mother.

Wayne bowed his head.

"God still has a plan for you," she said. "I know that. I believe it. I have to believe…that this struggle…hasn't been in vain." As she spoke, her words trailed off to a strengthless whisper, barely audible.

Tears came unbidden to his eyes. With an effort, Wayne forced them away. He cleared his throat. "It's been so hard. So hard."

"And you've doubted."

He nodded, gritting his teeth against a surge of emotion and shame. He pushed out the words: "Yes. God help me, I have."

"I know. I've seen it in your eyes. But you listen. From someone standing…at death's door. There is a reason. A plan. And the plan…is not for you to be cut down by some gang of thugs."

He wiped at his eyes. "If…if you say so."

"Look at me."

Though he feared looking into her eyes once more might shatter him, he obeyed. He trembled with the effort he exerted to keep from breaking down, then and there. He would not have her last memory of him be one of despair.

Her breathing had become even more labored. He wanted to tell her to rest, not to tax herself so, but he knew the futility of it. She would have her say.

"I won't last the night. I feel it in me, Wayne, and I have no strength left to fight it. I doubt…I'll even make it to sundown. I'll be gone before they get here. And so will you."

Denials rose to his lips, an automatic response, but faded away before he could so much as open his mouth. He recognized the truth when he heard it, a truth he could no longer hold at bay.

"I don't want you to die alone," he said.

She exhaled, took his hand. "I won't be alone. Melinda will be with me. And Robert. And Deborah. And the grandchildren. They're with me now. I feel…their presence. I'll be at peace…if I know that you're safe."

Her voice had become ragged. He squeezed her hand gently. He had no words.

"I'm going to close my eyes…for a bit. When I open them again…*if* I open them again…I don't want to see you."

Though her voice was almost gone, still her tone brooked no dissent.

"Believe me, Wayne Burleson: if you come to the hereafter so soon after me…I will make you wish you'd gone to hell."

"I believe you."

"Good." She released his hand, closed her eyes. "Now go."

He sat for long moments, watching her chest rise and fall, rise and fall. On another cot, a man continued wailing for his mother. The overhead lights flickered, went out, then came back on.

Wayne pulled his mask down, leaned over, and kissed Kathleen's forehead. Her skin was very warm, the fever burning the life out of her. "Goodbye, heart," he whispered.

He left her then, walking out of the hospital and never looking back.

He was some fifteen miles out of Nowata when his grief overtook him. He didn't bother pulling over; the road was deserted but for him. He just stopped the truck and gripped the steering wheel as violent shudders wracked him. A flood of tears obliterated his vision. Sounds came out of him that he could not recognize as human. The pain in his chest squeezed so hard that his breath came only in gasps. He tasted bitterness and salt.

An unknown time later, the storm receded. His hands ached, hooked into stiff claws on the steering wheel. Relaxing his grip took real effort.

He remembered looking out his dusty windshield. The sun had hung low in the western sky, nearing the horizon. Its cold beauty recked nothing of his cares. For all he'd known in that moment, his Kathleen was already gone, the last thing he cared about in the world, and he was alone.

He had put the truck back into gear and headed home, to await whatever would come next.

His feet burned by the time he finally came across what he assumed was H40—a dilapidated track running east-west, no longer worthy to be called a road. On a guess, he turned west, figuring that if he didn't come across Robin and Esteban in a mile or so, he'd head the other way.

He found the truck and trailer at the bottom of the next hill, angled half on and half off the road. He pulled out his flashlight and shone it around. As Serena had promised, the truck's tires had been shot out, all four of them. Wayne suppressed a curse. Two would have been enough.

He walked around the trailer, noted it had been padlocked shut, but saw no sign of Robin and Esteban. Good. They had heard him coming and had hidden themselves. No doubt they were watching him, weapons at the ready. He raised his hands and spoke to the darkness: "It's me. I'm alone."

Rustling behind him. Robin and Esteban emerged from a roadside ditch. Robin had her pistol, Esteban a rifle. Robin holstered her weapon but remained in place. Esteban set the rifle barrel on one shoulder and came over to Wayne, shook his hand. "Good to see you."

"Likewise. I could use some water, though."

"*Sí*. I'll get you some." Esteban headed for the trailer, fumbling at his belt for his keys as he went.

"We didn't know what to do," Robin said, still keeping her distance.

"You did the right thing."

"You were gone so long. I was starting to think that you'd been shot down…or that you weren't coming." She spoke in a monotone.

"It's much harder deflating and storing a balloon on your own."

"Where's the *Night Wind*?"

"Hidden. About two miles north of here."

Esteban returned from the trailer with another water bottle. "*Gracias*," Wayne said as he took it and drank greedily. The worst of his exhaustion fell from him.

"They took Jaime," Robin said. "Four of them. They were on us before we even knew they were here, and they took Jaime away. They would have taken all three of us if they could, but Esteban and I drew our weapons when they first moved in. They had a gun to his head. We couldn't stop them."

Wayne nodded. "They're holding him hostage. I spoke with him over the radio. He's alive. Safe."

Esteban absorbed this in silence, his features inscrutable in the darkness.

"Safe," Robin said, still deadpan. "That's comforting. What are they gonna do with him?"

"Hold him until I give them what they want." He briefly recounted Serena's demands.

"What a bitch." But the words fell out of Robin's mouth with no force, as emotionless as if she were commenting on the weather. She was still in shock.

"Yes," Wayne said. He became uncomfortably aware of Esteban's steady stare.

"So now what?" Robin said.

"Now we make camp and get some sleep. It's been a very long night for all of us. I don't know about you, but I'm ready to fall over."

"And what about Jaime?"

He sighed, his aching bones crying out for respite. "We can do nothing for him tonight. You're smart enough to know that, Robin."

"And what will we do in the morning?"

"Ask me in the morning."

She took a step toward him. "I have an idea."

"Wonderful. Let's discuss it after—"

"I think we need to discuss it now." She nodded toward Esteban. "*We* think we need to discuss it now. And you're not gonna like it."

The iron in her voice hinted that she perhaps wasn't in shock, after all. Wayne glanced from Esteban to Robin. They both stood firm, legs apart as if braced for action. No slumping or downcast gazes. She kept one hand on the butt of her pistol; Esteban still had his rifle resting against his shoulder.

Tension wound in his muscles again; he fancied he could hear his body groaning with the unwelcome exertion. "What are you—"

"Pay the ransom," she said.

"I beg your pardon?"

"Give Serena Katz what she wants. Then we get Jaime and get the hell out of here."

"We can't do that."

"Of course we can."

"You don't understand. You don't know what's going on in Plattsmouth."

"I don't ca—"

"They have a vaccine for the Red Death."

That stopped her cold.

He related his deductions, and Serena's tacit confirmation of them. "She's gearing up to make a stand against Plattsmouth. If I help her, I become an accomplice. It will only get people killed." He swigged more water from the bottle, then replaced the cap. "I won't do that."

Esteban's stance remained unchanged; Wayne wondered how much the man had understood. Robin, looked northward, toward Glenwood and its castle. Her shoulders heaved as her rate of breath increased. He'd seen her do that before; she was working herself up, getting angry.

She faced him again. "If these two little pissant towns are planning to start a miniature war, that's all the more reason to get out of here before it happens! Jesus, Wayne, can't you see that?"

He covered his eyes with one hand. "Did you even hear what I said, Robin? Just across the river, there's a vaccine for the Red Death. The rebuilding process has begun. This nightmare we've been living for years—it's almost over."

"Oh, Jee-*zus*, Wayne."

He dropped his hand and scowled. "I've told you before that I don't appreciate that kind of lang—"

She jabbed a finger in his direction. "I don't give a *shit* what you appreciate! Jaime's been abducted by some madwoman with delusions of grandeur, and you're talking about the nightmare ending? Personally, I think the nightmare's just getting started."

Bitterness flooded Wayne's mouth. "Do you know who you sound like right now? That madwoman with delusions of grandeur."

"You go to hell."

"We're not going to abandon Jaime." He spoke as much to Esteban as to her. "We're going to get him back. But I will not bargain with that woman for his life. She's given us no indication that she's trustworthy. Quite the opposite, in fact. Do you really think you can negotiate with a person like that?"

"She's holding all the cards! What choice do we have?"

"The choice we've always had. The road we've been on. We stand. We fight."

"We fight? With *what*? Some rifles and pistols, and an abandoned hot-air balloon that will probably be gone by morning? And just to refresh your memory, Wayne, we haven't been fighting at all! We've been inciting others to do that. We've been hiding in the shadows. Because that's all we *can* do. You've said yourself that a balloon isn't worth a shit in battle."

Wayne hung his head. "I know."

"So how would we get Jaime back?"

He looked up. "Ask me in the morning."

"You don't have any idea, do you?"

Wayne turned from her and started walking toward the trailer. He'd had all he could stomach from her tonight.

Esteban moved to intercept him. "No, *Señor* Wayne. We're not done talking." He pulled his rifle barrel off his shoulder and held the weapon with both hands.

Wayne became wary. He carried a sidearm, of course, but Esteban had the drop on him. And Robin stood at his back.

"What is this?" he said. "Some kind of mutiny? Are *you* challenging my authority now?"

"I am Jaime's father, *señor*. That's all the authority I need. Listen to the girl."

An illegal alien and a lesbian, telling him what to do. He had half a mind to explain to them a bit about America, make them see—

No. That was his exhaustion talking. And at a moment like this, such recklessness could lead to…irreversible action.

Wayne backed up a step, faced Robin. "Say what you have to say."

"Do you know why I joined up with you, Wayne? It wasn't because of your personality or your politics, that's for sure."

"Why, then?"

"When you came to Liberal, you brought us hope. Hope for the future. And let me tell you, that's been in short supply since the Red Death."

Ah, Liberal. Now *that* had been a liberation. Everything had gone just as it should have. He had flown reconnaissance, given his intel to the resistance, and let them do the rest. Rarely in his life had he been prouder. Tough, brave souls in that town. The victory over the thugs that had taken over there had been swift and certain. Robin had been so impressed that she'd asked to join his team, and the townspeople had gifted him with a lovely .38 revolver in gratitude. He'd drilled Robin on basic marksmanship, survival skills, and hot air balloon maintenance, and though she'd often grumbled, she'd stuck with it…and him.

"But over the last several weeks," she said, "I've started to have my doubts about you. We all have. I'm not so sure you're in this to bring hope. I've begun to think that all this"—she gestured toward him, then toward the trailer—"this grand plan of yours is just some expression of your vanity. That *you're* the one with delusions of grandeur. Like you're trying to remake the world the way you think it should be."

He wanted to ask her if she had learned that in some college psych class but thought the better of it.

"And now, with Jaime in trouble, you say you won't pay the ransom. I think that's just an excuse. I think maybe the real reason is that you just don't want to knuckle under to anybody, no matter the cost." She brushed a few stray strands of hair from her face. "Your pride could very well get Jaime killed, and this war between Plattsmouth and Glenwood will still happen."

Wayne glanced over his shoulder at Esteban, then back to Robin. "So you want me to give Serena what she's asking for, and just hope that she'll honor her word, is that it?"

"I—yes. That's it."

"And if I don't, what happens?"

"We're not really asking, Wayne."

"You're the one giving the orders now, then?"

She looked heavenward for a moment. "God, you can be such a little boy sometimes. Look, since you love America so much, let's be democratic about it. I say we cooperate with Serena and get Jaime back. Those in favor?" She raised her hand.

Esteban came from behind Wayne and stood beside Robin, his hand up, too.

"Those opposed?"

The two of them lowered their hands. Wayne only stood there, facing them.

"The ayes have it," she said.

"Congratulations. And will you two gun me down if I don't obey?"

"You know, I think you might actually enjoy that." Her voice dripped bile. "But no, making you a martyr won't help Jaime. We can't force you, and you know it." She stepped toward him, spoke in a gentler tone: "Look, I don't like it, either. But living to fight another day—there's nobility in that, too. Come on, Wayne. Be reasonable."

He regarded her with mingled wonder and contempt. How adult she sounded in that moment...and how smug. She was more like Serena than she knew.

She would get the same answer, then. He cleared his throat and said, "I don't negotiate with terrorists."

Robin exchanged glances with Esteban. "What did you say?"

"You heard me. And I'm not negotiating with you, either. If that upsets you, I'm well beyond caring. The last thing Jaime said to me before they cut him off was not to give in to Serena. He understands, better than either of you, about honor and integrity. We *will* get him back, but not this way. That's my final word on the matter. Now if there's nothing else, I'm going to make camp."

He started for the trailer, but Esteban's voice stopped him: "Not here, you're not."

Wayne looked back at them. Esteban had raised his rifle, seated its butt against his shoulder, and drawn a bead on him. "I want my son back. If you weren't such a stubborn *pendejo*, he would never have been taken. It's your fault, *comprende*? Your fault. If you won't help make it right, you don't make camp with us."

Wayne raised his hands. "May I at least take my backpack?"

"Yes. But not any food or water."

Robin looked to Esteban. "Are you sure about—"

"We worked for it, in Glenwood. It's ours. He can get his own." Even as he spoke, he kept the rifle aimed and ready.

"Fine," Wayne said.

Esteban lowered his weapon a little, tossed the trailer keys to Robin. She unlocked it. With the two of them watching, Wayne climbed inside. The trailer had much more space in it with the *Night Wind* gone. Its emptiness struck a sad chord in him. He ignored it and collected his backpack. He climbed out and slipped the straps over his shoulders. The familiar weight settled in.

To Robin, he said, "What will you do?"

"The only thing we can do—wait for you to come around. Don't make us wait too long, though. Jaime's life depends on it."

"You can't leave this trailer out here. Sooner or later—"

"Let us worry about that."

"We're still being hunted, remember," he said.

"Believe me, I know."

"Be careful."

"You, too. Hope to see you in the morning, Wayne."

"Don't count on it."

With that, he walked away from them, heading east.

CHAPTER FOUR

IRREVERSIBLE ACTION

He didn't walk very far—maybe another half mile away, just enough to get out of their sight. His legs strained to carry him; he called upon his deepest reserves to push himself on the final stretch. His arthritis, normally manageable, punished him with every step, a harbinger of what he would face the next day. Anger and disbelief warred within him, slowing his steps.

He made camp among the roadside trees, his smoothly efficient routine hampered by darkness, exhaustion, and aching joints. Once inside his bedroll, the ground hard, cold, and lumpy beneath him, he tumbled immediately into sleep.

Sunlight awakened him. From the inside of his tent, the shadows of trees stood out in clear relief. Judging from the angle, he estimated the time at eight o'clock.

As he feared, the stiffness in his joints verged on paralysis. Even stretching drew long groans from him. Just extricating himself from the sleeping bag became a difficult and painful enterprise. He gritted his teeth and forced his way through it. He had much to do, and no time to lose.

The day had dawned clear and cold. Light frost lay on the ground as he emerged from the tent. A sky of crystalline blue arched overhead. Though the chill in the air did nothing to improve his aching bones—he lurched through his morning routine on legs that refused to bend, hobbled by a spine that refused to straighten—it nonetheless invigorated him. Autumn had always been his favorite time of year, even as a child.

He clamped down on that line of thinking. Memories of his past, of his time before the Red Death, were dangerous things. He knew from past experience that longing for all he had lost could paralyze him more thoroughly than his worst day of arthritis.

Neither could he afford to mourn the loss of Jaime, and the suddenness with which Robin and Esteban had turned against him. The confrontation with Robin had been a long time coming, but that in itself he could have handled. Esteban's betrayal, on the other hand, rankled and hurt. Perhaps Wayne's expectations of the man had been too high.

Though acutely aware of time passing, Wayne forced himself to perform a series of painful stretches and exercises. He would need full mobility today; cowering in his tent and waiting for the pain to pass was not an option. As he worked, Robin's words came back to him. *Some expression of your vanity*, she had called it. *Like you're trying to remake the world the way you think it should be.*

Well, who *didn't* try to remake the world? Only two types—the complacent and the timid. He had no patience with either. If that was vanity, let it be vanity.

I've started to have my doubts about you. We all have.

That hurt, too—the notion that they'd been discussing him behind his back.

Fallout from Independence, of course. He had never promised them this road would be easy, but their earlier successes had softened them a bit, leaving them unprepared when genuine adversity hit.

Like Independence. Captain Dark Eagle's first—and to date, only—failure.

Just east of the ruins of Kansas City, Independence had come under the thumb of a ruthless militia run by a man who called himself Jack Knife, a lunatic who resembled nothing so much as a deranged Viking—barrel-chested and beefy, with long red hair and even longer beard. Knife and his band of thugs had been holed up in an old courthouse, making aerial reconnaissance tricky. At the very least, though, Dark Eagle had been able to map their sentry positions outside the building, an easy task with the night vision binoculars. Then he'd handed off the maps and diagrams he'd drawn up to a group of young, grim idealists determined to free the city, wished them Godspeed, and flew off—back to the abandoned farmhouse outside of town where he and his team were staying, there to await news of the eventual victory.

Something had gone wrong.

Maybe Dark Eagle had overlooked one of the sentry positions. Or maybe the people of Independence didn't get to all of them in time. Wayne never knew exactly what had happened. The best he could piece together from garbled radio transmission was that the attack on the courthouse had been thwarted, many of the would-be freedom fighters had been captured, and an enraged Jack Knife had sent his men on a rampage. Rebel corpses—skinned, broken, and mutilated—had been hung up outside the courthouse for all to see.

Some of them had apparently talked under torture, had given up everyone who'd been involved in the attack. At least one of them must have mentioned that they'd been aided by a crazy old man in a black hot-air balloon.

When Wayne and his team decided to flee, they ran into a roadblock—two jeeps, black with bright flame jobs across their hoods, parked nose-to-nose across the highway.

They'd attempted to talk their way through, but Jack Knife himself had been there, had insisted on inspecting the trailer.

Esteban and Robin each took out one of Knife's goons before the firefight could begin in earnest. Wayne, for his part, managed to tag Knife in the knee. He'd bellowed as he'd fallen, and his gaze met Wayne's—just for an instant, but it was enough. Jack Knife bared his teeth. Though Wayne was dressed in civilian clothes, the two of them knew each other in that moment.

Knife had pointed, accusatory. "Dark Eagle!"

With their leader down, the rest of the armed goons hesitated. Robin slammed the truck in gear and barreled around the roadblock. Somehow, she managed the maneuver without tipping the trailer. Esteban and Jaime tossed a pair of Molotov cocktails from their weapons store at the jeeps, discouraging pursuit.

They'd escaped with their lives, which was more than Wayne could say for many others that day. But the damage had been done, both to Independence and to his team. Fleeing defeat gnawed at each of them; he could see it in a slight stoop of the shoulders, hear it in pregnant silences around their campfires. Worse still, Jack Knife was the only man alive, outside of his own team, who had knowingly laid eyes on the unmasked face of Captain Dark Eagle.

They'd sped north on Interstate 29, spending their nights in the hills, far off the road. Whenever they came out of seclusion to barter for supplies, they heard rumors of some unsavory characters from the south asking after an old man and three companions who drove around a black trailer.

When they'd come across the first sign from Glenwood, Wayne had taken it as a sign from God that they'd at last outrun Jack Knife's wrath and were to resume their liberation work. Then they could wash the bitterness of Independence from their mouths, and perhaps find a place to hole up for the winter.

Served him right for thinking he knew the mind of the Almighty.

The stretching exercises allowed him some limited mobility. It was a start. His joints and muscles would loosen up more as he got further into the day. He hoped.

He inventoried his backpack. The food he had in there—nuts, bread, apples, some salted meat—would last him another couple of days, and his ranger training would aid him with hunting and foraging. Water would be easy enough to come by, this close to the river. Drinking directly from it wouldn't be his first option, but he would boil the water before he drank it, anyway…and even then, it would taste awful.

Ammunition, by contrast, would be much harder to come by, and he was running low.

Not that he would need any of it today, if all went according to plan.

The sun rose above the trees as he worked. His own reckoning put the time at around nine o'clock. Most of the frost had disappeared, but the chill in the air lingered. The temperature wouldn't get much above forty. The walk he had ahead of him would warm him up.

He broke down camp and moved out, heading west.

His arthritis slowed him, but the stretches paid some dividends. The pain subsided to a dull ache, easily tuned out. That was good, because he had a long hike ahead of him—at least ten miles, probably more. At his current pace, that would take over two hours. He thanked God that the weather had cooperated.

He saw no other living soul along the way. The grassy plains, mostly brown with lateness of the season, spread from horizon to horizon in every direction. Occasional flocks of migrating birds flew overhead, including a honking V of geese, but other than that, the land was silent and empty. That was nothing new, of course; the world had gotten awfully quiet since the Red Death. Wayne usually enjoyed the peace. He considered it one of the few good things that had come of the plague. America had been such a dadgum noisy, frenetic place in the old days. For whatever reason, though, as he made his way down County Road H40, the stillness struck him as somehow eerie, as if the countryside were a giant, open-air tomb.

It occurred to him that he hadn't been this alone in a long time, since the Red Death had taken away everyone he loved and for some inexplicable reason left him alive. The realization brought with it a pang that struck him harder than he would have suspected possible. He was concerned for Jaime, naturally, and he had come to rely on Esteban, even if the man was an illegal. But Robin—

That hotheaded girl stood as a walking affront to so much that he believed in and live by. He'd never dreamed he would miss her insolence and defiance…but he did.

"Silly old man," he said under his breath. "Focus."

He contemplated the next few hours. This course of action was fraught with danger. It would behoove him to have some contingency plan in place, in case something went wrong. Nothing came to mind.

He reached the interstate and turned north for a few miles, then west again. He knew this part of the hike well; he'd walked it only a few days previous.

The sun had moved past zenith by the time he arrived once more at the Plattsmouth bridge. The trek had taken him much longer than he would have liked. It couldn't be entirely attributed to his arthritis slowing him down; he must have underestimated the distance.

He estimated the span at a quarter mile. The design of the bridge looked very old, even antiquated. Even at a distance, the rust on the iron trusses was apparent. The structure would not have looked out of place at the turn of the previous century. That it still stood at all was something of a miracle. The trusses hadn't even been scavenged.

The pavement, though, looked normal—or, rather, it looked like something that had once been normal. Smooth, devoid of potholes, neatly patched—the roadwork he had observed the other day.

He walked past the quarantine sign and stepped onto the bridge, holding the straps of his backpack as he walked, maintaining a steady pace, doing what he could to project confidence and nonchalance.

Below him, the land sloped gently away toward the river. The brown water flowed sluggishly, smelling of fish and sewage. On the far side of the bridge stood a small structure—a toll booth. Beyond that, the road wound into tall, foliage-covered hills, leading to the city of Plattsmouth.

The bridge stood quiet and deserted. He raised his hands as he stepped onto it, moving slowly, giving the sentries no excuse to open fire. Not that they needed one. It would be simple enough matter to gun him down and dump his body into the river. But the sentries were trained soldiers, and he knew how to talk to them. He counted on them being disciplined, honorable, accountable to a chain of command. He was betting his life on it, in fact.

Nothing happened until he reached the halfway point of the bridge: “Halt!”

Wayne obeyed, and two figures carrying rifles emerged from the toll booth. He had no way of telling whether these were the same two he'd observed the other day.

The one on Wayne's left, with a prominent widow's peak and bearing a bit of paunch around the middle, waggled his rifle. “This bridge is closed. Turn around and go back to Glenwood.”

“I need to speak to your CO.”

The two exchanged glances. The one on the left spoke again: “What did you say?”

“Your CO, please. I need to speak to him. Or her.”

“No. That's not possible. Turn around. Now.”

“I'm giving myself up. You can search me if you like. I have a .38 in my holster, and a rifle in my backpack.” He considered.

"Oh, and a hunting knife, too. Those are my only weapons. I'm perfectly willing to hand them over in order to gain entrance. I know you'll take good care of them."

The one on the right—a younger man, maybe Jaime's age, with cropped red hair and a prominent Adam's apple—advanced a step and said, "Who are you? We don't have any work, if that's what you're looking for."

"Wayne Burleson is my name. I'm not looking for work. I have important information for your CO."

"I'm sure," the one on the left said. The older of the two, he would be senior. "Tell us what your information is, and we'll decide whether or not it's important."

Wayne smiled and slowly shook his head. "I'm afraid that's for your CO only."

Both sentries chuckled. "Sorry, then," the older one said. "Turn around and head back now."

"Are you with the 55th?" Wayne asked.

"Beg pardon?"

"The 55th Wing." He nodded northward. "From Offutt."

"We're not Air Force," the younger one said.

"Good," Wayne said. "I heard the 55th was nothing but a bunch a candy asses." He offered a silent prayer of forgiveness for the profanity.

That got a genuine laugh from both of them. "Yeah, I've heard that, too," said the senior.

"First Infantry Division?"

"You know it. Still the Big Red One. Sixteenth Regiment."

Wayne nodded. "Worked with them a few times. Got an important job to do, you need to bring in the right people."

"What about you, Burleson? Infantry?"

"Ranger. Retired."

"Your accent says you're not from around here. Sounds southern."

"Oklahoma."

"And you've hiked all the way to Nebraska?"

"I've gotten some rides, too. But I like walking."

"You won't like it very much once the snow starts flying."

"That's true."

The senior's posture relaxed a little. He let the rifle barrel drop.

"Well, listen, Ranger. We can't let you through. You should know that. We have orders."

"Of course you do. All I'm asking is that you call it in."

"And tell them what? That you have important information?"

"Concerning Glenwood."

The sentries exchanged glances again. The senior said, "Glenwood, eh? So they're seriously gonna take a run at us?"

"Maybe not, if I can talk to your CO."

The senior stared at Wayne for long moments, then looked to his partner. "All right, call it in. I'll keep an eye on our Ranger friend here."

CHAPTER FIVE

STRANGE AND UNCERTAIN TIMES

While the junior sentry spoke into his radio, the senior allowed Wayne to put his arms down—after having him set aside the .38 and his backpack, which the sentry inspected before laying it on the ground next to the weapon. Wayne and he stood at ease on the bridge, leaning against trusses and looking out over the Missouri flowing beneath them. They spoke little.

Wayne wondered how well stocked with vaccine these people were. They'd already ranged a goodly distance from Offutt Air Force Base. Presumably, they'd secured and vaccinated any survivors in that area before moving south. At some point, new supplies would have to be flown in.

Then again, the Red Death had hit the bigger cities hardest, turning them into charnel pits. Probably not much call for the vaccine in and around Omaha.

Well, he would have answers to all his questions about the forces occupying Plattsmouth soon enough. Everything he knew about them had come from Serena Katz, and she had proven herself untrustworthy. Plattsmouth was a leap of faith, and his best remaining option.

"I'll tell you this much," the senior said. "Even *if* they decide to let you through, it's not gonna be very pleasant. No one's gonna risk breaking quarantine for you."

"Wouldn't expect them to."

The younger sentry approached a few minutes later. "It's being referred up the chain." To Wayne, he said, "You'll have to stay here. No going forward, no going back."

"Naturally." The news encouraged him. He no longer doubted that they would let him in. They would make him wait a while—probably several hours, if past experience with the army was any guide—but eventually, they would let him pass. Really, winding through any military bureaucracy required patience and persistence beyond all reason. Once they finally understood that you weren't going away, that they would have to deal with you sooner or later, only then would anything get done.

So when a boxy armored truck came rumbling down the winding road from Plattsmouth less than an hour later, Wayne's surprise verged on shock. The truck stopped next to the toll booth. A red cross had been painted on its gray exterior, making it resemble an ambulance. The junior sentry's radio crackled, and a tinny voice said, "All right, bring him over."

The senior sentry picked up Wayne's backpack and .38, and the three of them walked to the ambulance. They went to the rear of the vehicle. The senior opened it, motioning Wayne inside. Wayne complied.

The interior was gray, windowless, and bare, without so much as a seat. The roof was low enough that he had to stoop. He saw no access to the cab.

The senior sentry still held Wayne's belongings. "I'll give these to the driver. They'll be returned to you after." He raised a hand to Wayne. "Good luck, Ranger."

The door slammed shut, leaving Wayne in darkness. He shrugged and sat cross-legged on the floor. Moments later, the truck jerked into gear and was off.

The ride took only a few minutes, for which Wayne was grateful. The rear of the truck had not been built for comfort, and its suspension system left much to be desired, even by military transport standards. He bounced and slid with each turn, unable to secure or brace himself.

His relief when the truck stopped was short-lived. The rear door opened again, and two soldiers in cammies, both brandishing M1 rifles, motioned him out. The one on the left had a soup-strainer mustache; the one on the right stood taller than Wayne by a head. "Out," the tall one said. "Move!"

Wayne emerged into a large garage area with a cracked concrete floor. The ambulance was the only truck there, though two more such vehicles could easily fit. A musty and dank smell hung in the air. Like the inside of the ambulance, the place had been stripped, empty of equipment or even clutter. To his left was a set of metal double doors inset with small windows of reinforced glass, bearing the legend *Cass County Correctional Facility* in cracked and peeling black paint.

As soon as he stepped off the truck, the soldiers grabbed him by the arms and urged him toward the doors. "Let's *go*, meat," the tall one said.

Once inside, they took him to the basement level, made him strip naked, and forced him into a decon shower that had been set up there. Water at near-scalding temperatures blasted him. An acrid smell told him that it had been laced with some kind of detergent. His skin burned, turning an angry red. He gritted his teeth against it, not allowing himself to groan or complain. The tall soldier kept his weapon trained on him throughout. The mustachioed one kept time with a stopwatch. Wayne knew better than to protest his good health at this point. These functionaries were just doing their job; he would get the full treatment no matter what. Uncooperativeness would only take longer. Even so, he reserved some white-hot hatred for the bastard with the stopwatch.

The shower seemed to last half an hour, though he knew that it had probably not exceeded five minutes. Afterward, they subjected him to an eyebath that took another minute or so. Then they shoved him, gasping for breath, skin and eyes still burning, into a wooden stall. Inside was a towel and a white jumpsuit. He dried off as best he could and donned the jumpsuit—some tough, synthetic material that covered him head to foot.

From there, they led him to a small examination room, white-walled, containing a pallet and a wheeled shelving unit full of medical equipment, most of it wrapped in plastic. The stopwatch soldier with the soup-strainer made him strip again, took his temperature and a blood sample, then closely examined his skin, no doubt looking for signs of the Red Death's telltale rash. He palpated Wayne's arms, legs, and midriff, probing for tender points. Wayne mentioned his arthritis, but the examiner only grunted in response. He gave brusque instructions throughout the procedure. The tall soldier loomed in one corner of the room, M1 at the ready.

Wayne remained compliant during the ordeal, but inwardly wondered how much of this was necessary, even for a quarantined area. His lack of a fever—the first sign of the Red Death, presenting within mere hours of infection—should have been enough to allay any fear that he was a carrier. The rest of the decon process struck him as overkill and a waste of resources. The cynic in him suspected that it had more to do with humiliation and subjugation than the prevention of infection.

After the exam, they threw him into a cell and told him that he would be cleared only if his bloodwork came through clean.

"How long will that take?" he asked.

"As long as it takes," the examiner said.

That white-hot hatred flared in Wayne again.

The two of them left him alone in the cell.

It was a simple eight by eight unit, one of four he could see from this vantage point, adorned only with a cot and a stainless steel toilet. Concrete block walls, cracked and crumbling in places, but still plenty solid, and bearing no signs of graffiti. The air down here smelled vaguely of antiseptic, with no trace of urine or must. They had done a thorough job of converting a county jail into a quarantine facility.

Next to the cot was a single bottle of water and a couple of sealed packets that Wayne recognized immediately—MRE rations. He couldn't help chuckling. Even after everything the country had been through, some things never changed.

Being neither hungry nor thirsty, only wiped out from the long hike and the decon, he stretched out on the cot. Despite its Spartan hardness, it was the most comfortable place he'd lain in—he thought back—at least two months.

Drowsiness stole over him, and he saw no point in fighting it. He dozed fitfully, drifting between half-remembered dreams and waking, with no clear distinction between the two.

A clanking startled him awake an unknown time later. Belatedly, he recognized it as the slam of a door. Approaching footsteps echoed off the concrete floor.

He got up slowly. The stiffness had settled in his joints again; he pushed through it, stood. The decon soldiers were back. The examiner unlocked and opened the cell door while the tall one kept his weapon trained on Wayne. The drill was getting a bit tired, but he refrained from making any ill-advised comments.

They led him past the decon station and back upstairs, down a long, twisty corridor to a small conference room, as stripped as the rest of the place. Fluorescent lighting overhead, a round wooden table, three office chairs with torn and faded green upholstery. The walls were clean and unadorned.

The tall one shoved him in, shut the door behind him. The click of a lock sounded.

Wayne stood for a moment, looking around the room. It was basically a box, only slightly friendlier than the cell. He peered at its corners for any sign of a camera or other surveillance device, saw only a couple of cobwebs. He took a seat and waited, hands folded in front of him on the table.

His stomach rumbled. He supposed he should have helped himself to one of the MRE rations they had provided, but his weariness had gotten the better of him.

By his own reckoning, half an hour elapsed before the door opened again. In strode a pair of uniformed men—one thin and totally bald, with an eagle insignia that identified him as a colonel, and the second shorter and bespectacled, carrying a note pad and some file folders, bearing a major's oak leaf.

Wayne stood and saluted.

The two officers glanced at each other, then returned the salute. The thin man wore a faint smile. He said, "I'm Colonel Nicholas Edwards. This is Major Oswald."

"Thank you for seeing me on such short notice, Colonel. I'm Wayne Burleson."

The major said, "Seventy-fifth Ranger Regiment, Second Battalion, correct?"

Wayne put down momentary alarm. The decon soldiers had undoubtedly noticed the Second Battalion tattoo on his right shoulder during the shower or subsequent examination. "That's correct, Major. Retired master sergeant."

"Terrific," Edwards said. "Shall we?" He gestured to the chairs.

They sat. Oswald set the notepad and file folders in front of him. He opened one of them and handed a sheet of paper to

Edwards. The colonel leaned back in his chair as he scanned the document, crossed his legs. "Well, Sergeant Burleson," he said, "the meds tell me you're clean, no sign of Red Death. Congratulations."

Wayne only nodded his acknowledgment.

"This report says that you were apprehended carrying a rifle, sidearm, and a hunting knife."

"I wasn't apprehended, Colonel," Wayne said. "I surrendered myself to you. I told the sentries about my weapons. It's basic survival gear, sir, nothing more."

Edwards flapped a hand, as if batting the words aside. "I can deduce all that on my own, Sergeant." He rattled the paper. "It also says you were carrying nothing that could be construed as an explosive device or gas weapon, no surveillance equipment, nothing that could pose a threat to this encampment."

"I'm not a danger to anyone here, Colonel."

"We'll see about that." Edwards set the report aside. Oswald opened a second folder, handed him some crumpled pages overlaid with close handwriting. "The only thing you were carrying that is of any interest to me is this." He leaned forward, laid the papers in the center of the table.

Wayne recognized them. They were his reconnaissance notes from the flight over the castle in Glenwood.

"Would you care to explain what this is and where you got it?" Edwards said.

"This is what I wanted to discuss with you." Wayne pointed out the map he had drawn. "What you see here, Colonel, is a map of a former resort hotel that Serena Katz has commandeered as her base of operations in Glenwood. It shows entry points"—he indicated them as he spoke—"sentry positions, and likely storage facilities and command center. These arrows indicate potential weaknesses that might be exploitable." He smoothed out the other sheets and turned them so that the officers could read them. "Here I've sketched out a battle plan that takes advantage of a blind spot on the western approach. You could—"

Edwards raised a hand. "Sergeant, I assure you, I can read."

"You asked me for an explanation, sir."

"You drew all this up yourself?"

"Yes, sir."

"Why?"

"You don't think it's useful?"

Edwards's features hardened. "Answer my question."

"Sir, I've had a run-in with these people. They've abducted a friend of mine, a young man named Jaime Gonzalez. I want him back, but I can't get him on my own. I also know, sir, that you're planning to, ah, secure Glenwood soon. I need your help, and it seems to me that you need this intelligence."

Edwards regarded him coolly, one hand tapping the table. "And what makes you think I'm planning to *secure* Glenwood?"

"Sir, everyone in Glenwood knows it."

Edwards looked to Oswald. "What do you think?"

The major shrugged. "It's an unusual story. If he were lying, I'd think it would be something much more prosaic."

"It's the truth, sir." As he spoke, though, Wayne got the distinct impression that they were toying with him.

Edwards clucked his tongue. "So. You've come here to trade this intelligence for your friend's rescue."

"Yes, sir. A small strike force could use this data to pull off the operation quickly, quietly, and with minimal casualties. It certainly beats going in blind."

"Awfully fortunate for us, then, that you came along."

"Fortunate for me, too, sir. As I said, I can't do it alone."

Edwards picked up the map again. "And exactly how were you able to get such a detailed diagram? Do you have access to some secret blueprints?"

"I have scout training."

"Scout training. I see." He flipped the map back onto the table. He rocked a little in his chair, eyes on Wayne.

Wayne's discomfort deepened. He cleared his throat. "Sir, if you want to act on this intelligence, you would—"

"Sergeant Burleson, among your equipment was a single two-way radio. Where's its companion?"

Edwards had a predatory gleam in his gaze, as if he expected to catch Wayne dissembling. But the truth was easier: "Serena Katz has it. She took it from Jaime."

"Your friend. The one she's holding captive."

"Yes, sir."

Edwards tapped the map. "And where did you get this, again?"

Wayne sensed a trap, became wary. "I drew it myself."

"You scouted the area."

"Yes, sir."

Edwards drew a long breath. "A former resort hotel, in the hills near Glenwood. Must have been some tricky work. The terrain would make mapping awfully difficult."

"I never claimed it was easy, sir."

Wayne expected the remark to anger Edwards, but the colonel only gave a small smile. "Well, that's a strange story you've told us, Sergeant. And I have to tell you, we've heard some pretty odd ones since coming out here. Haven't we, Oswald?"

The major nodded. "Yes, we have, sir."

"In fact, just a few days ago, we apprehended some men who tried to gain entrance at the southern checkpoint. They warned us that a crackpot terrorist is working in this area. An older man wearing a mask and going around in a hot air balloon. He apparently firebombed the town of Independence, Missouri, about a month or so ago, which resulted in over fifty deaths."

Wayne's wariness blossomed into outright alarm. He saw where Edwards was going now. And his blood boiled at the mention of a *crackpot terrorist.*

"I dismissed the story when I heard it," Edwards said. "Until three nights ago, when Plattsmouth was buzzed in the middle of the night by a black hot air balloon."

Wayne stiffened, knowing it probably showed, but unable to stop himself. He clamped down on his anger before it could get out of hand. These two men sat between him and the door. No way he could get past them.

"And now you show up here, carrying a map that looks like it was made from the air." Edward's gaze sharpened. "Strange, indeed, but these are strange and uncertain times, aren't they, Oswald?"

"Yes, sir." The major stood, went to the door, opened it. To someone in the hall outside, he said, "Come in."

Slow, shuffling footsteps approached. A large figure came into view. Major Oswald stepped aside.

Wayne found himself looking upon the face of Jack Knife.

The deranged eyes and full beard hadn't changed one bit. The only difference Wayne noted was that the bastard now walked with a cane.

Knife saw him and lunged. Oswald caught his arm. "Easy, cowboy. Back down."

Knife obeyed, his baleful gaze fixed on Wayne. The lunge could only have been for show, anyway. Hobbled, Knife certainly couldn't move very fast. And if he'd been serious about getting to Wayne, he would have barreled through Oswald.

Edwards glanced back at Knife. "Well?"

"That's him," Knife said. "That's the one, General."

Edwards winced. "Thanks for the promotion, Jack, but I'm afraid only the President can do that. I'll remain just a colonel for now."

"Colonel," Wayne said, "whatever this man has told you is a lie. *He's* the one responsible for the deaths in Independence. He and his band of thugs have instituted a bloody reign of terror down there. He—"

"You shut your mouth!" Knife lunged again, and this time Oswald strained to hold him back. "Let me have him, Colonel! I'll shut his lying mouth for good. I'll—"

"*Quiet.*" Edwards said it with simple, cold command, something Wayne had heard only from the most seasoned of officers. Knife stopped himself, settled back. Oswald kept a hand on his arm.

"You leave him to us, Jack," Edwards said. "We're not a bunch of savages here. Strange though the times may be, this is still America, and we'll handle this like Americans. You go tell your men to get ready. They'll move in tonight."

Knife grumbled, long and low, like a growl. He pointed at Wayne. "You're getting off easy, Dark Eagle. If it were up to me, you'd die in agony." He turned and hobbled away. Oswald motioned to someone else outside the room. A moment later, two armed guards stood in the doorway.

Wayne gaped at Edwards. "You're sending *his* men into Glenwood? Those butchers?"

The colonel stood. "Strange and uncertain times, Sergeant…or should I say *Captain*?" He gave another small smile. "We have to pick our battles. Our resources aren't infinite." He picked up Wayne's reconnaissance notes. "One makes do with what one has."

"And how are you paying them, Colonel? Do they get to keep whatever spoils they get from Glenwood?"

Edwards glowered. "There will be no spoils. Suffice to say that those men owe us."

Wayne understood. "You've already vaccinated them, haven't you?"

Edwards and Oswald exchanged a glance. "I beg your pardon?" Edwards said.

"Never mind." Wayne sagged in his chair. "You're making a huge mistake, Colonel."

"I'll be the judge of that." Edwards handed the papers to Oswald, who tucked them back into one of his folders. "Now then, this young friend of yours, this"—he snapped his fingers, searching for the name—"this *Jaime*. I assume he's one of your team. How many others do you have in your little operation? Where might we find them?"

Through numb lips, Wayne replied automatically: "I don't have a team. I work alone."

"Of course. Wouldn't have it any other way, would we, Oswald?"

The major glanced in Wayne's direction. "Not at all, sir."

"I want to know what you learned when you overflew Plattsmouth," Edwards said, "and how many other people know it. I want every scrap of intelligence you've gleaned about this area. And I want to know how many more of you terrorists are out there. You can tell me now, or you can tell me later. But one way or another, you will tell me. Think it over, Captain.

"Thank you; that will be all."

He and Oswald left. The guards came in to escort Wayne back to his cell.

CHAPTER SIX

IMPLIED ORDERS

He paced in his cage relentlessly, unable to stop, despite the aching and swelling in his hips and knees. It was the only thing that kept him from grabbing the bars and baying like an animal, his way of outrunning the rage that threatened to overtake him.

It had been a long time since he'd felt so helpless, so hopeless, a long time since his madness had lurked so close to the surface.

Robin's voice spoke in his mind, sneering and sardonic: *Oh, yeah? You take to the skies as a masked avenger named Captain Dark Eagle, and you think the madness is* below *the surface?*

He pounded a fist on the bars, ignoring the pain, and continued pacing.

A long time. Not since Kathleen's death.

Wayne had little memory of those weeks. He had thought that his breakdown on the road would be a one-time loss of control. But he seemed to recall other outbursts, coming at damnably unpredictable moments—walking into a room and expecting to see Kathleen there, or preparing a meal and realizing that he only needed one plate, or, worst of all, just upon waking, when his defenses were at the weakest. He would rise to consciousness, momentarily certain that Kathleen would be in the bed next to him, that the entire Red Death and the loss of his family had been only a bad dream he'd finally escaped, and that blissful normalcy awaited him when opened his eyes. But her side of the bed would always be empty, and the morning sun streaming in through the blinds, a normally welcome sight, seemed somehow cold and accusatory, even threatening.

His sleep cycle became deeply irregular. Some days, he would awake to find the bedroom dark and the sun setting, every muscle sore. On others, he would lie in bed for hours, physically exhausted and aching, the arthritis gnawing at him, but unable to quiet his thoughts. He still had some medication in the bathroom, but refused to take it, knowing that what his supply was likely all he would ever have.

He remembered passing endless hours sitting on the front porch, his rifle laid across his knees, ignoring the chill of late winter, gazing across the acreage and the winding gravel driveway leading to the road. The last of the snow was gone, and already the yard had begun to green again. Now was the time for cleanup and tilling, preparing the gardens for the arrival of spring. He had seeds laid by in the pantry—tomatoes, beans, lettuce, carrots, many others—and he would need fresh produce more than he ever had in his life. The freeze and thaw cycle had done its normal damage to the driveway; he usually did the patching and grading himself, and this year he would have no choice. He knew that he would be much healthier and happier keeping his mind and body occupied.

Instead, he sat on the porch and thought of Kathleen.

He wondered what they had done with her body. Had they given her a decent burial, erected a small cross to at least mark her final resting place? Had they cremated her? Tossed her ignominiously into a mass grave, like the ones he had seen on the news just before general broadcasts ceased? Or had they simply left her and the rest of the victims to rot in that hospital basement?

Anger would surge through him then—at God, at the Red Death, at the incompetent government officials who had let everything fall apart on their watch…and, yes, even at Kathleen.

Bad enough that she had gotten herself sick, despite his constant warnings to take every precaution against infection. Certainly *he* had been careful, hadn't he? But even worse, by sending him away, she had robbed him of the opportunity to properly mourn her. He hadn't been there to comfort her in her final last moments. He'd had no funeral for her, no memorial. He couldn't even say a prayer over her grave. How could he move on without at least some ceremony to mark her passing?

He could only sit, alone and miserable, and watch as the days melted one into the next. Him, Wayne Burleson, retired Army Ranger, skilled hot air balloon pilot, a model of toughness and self-sufficiency. He had never asked for a favor in his life, had forged his own destiny, had reaped the rewards of faith, courage, and hard work. And he'd been reduced to this, a mindless automaton, helpless as a child, like all the whiners he had encountered in his years, the ones who blamed everyone else for their problems, who always expected to have the world handed to them.

He sometimes thought of the ballooning equipment in the garage, neatly stowed in a black trailer. He hadn't been up in some time. The urge to fly tugged at him, to flee this place and all of its attendant memories, to let the wind take him where it would. But sooner or later, he would have to come back down. Takeoffs were optional, landings mandatory. The idea of ballooning filled him only with despair.

And he realized that he was angry at himself, worst of all. But not even self-loathing could motivate him. It seemed so pointless anymore.

In those moments, he would glance at the rifle in his lap and consider looking straight down its barrel. Only his promise to Kathleen stopped him.

Somewhere beyond the acreage, the world moved on. Out there, people were struggling and dying. Civilization was busy eating itself. None of it seemed to matter. He could make a reasonably comfortable life for himself here, he knew. Oklahoma winters were comparatively mild, and he was more than capable of securing provisions enough to survive them. He could survive, maybe even thrive, ignoring whatever remained of society, untroubled by the concerns of other people. He could wait it out, until death, long delayed, finally came for him.

But that probably hadn't been what Kathleen had had in mind when she'd told him that there was still a plan for him.

The weeks wore on, winter giving way to early spring. His beard came in, thick and white. He drifted, on some days going through the motions of a normal life, on others just waiting for all of it to end.

In his darkest moments, he doubted even Kathleen's final words to him. Maybe there was no plan. Maybe he hadn't been spared for a reason. Maybe he hadn't even been as careful as he'd supposed. Maybe he'd just been lucky—if that was the right word.

Wayne worked to dismiss the memories, hazy and indistinct though they were. He'd lost all track of time since being stuck in this cell. It seemed like at least twelve hours, though he knew it had probably been much less than that. Dwelling on it would only make him crazy…or crazier. He had to focus on what he could do, what he could control.

Robin spoke in his mind again: *At the moment, that would be nothing, Wayne. Not a damned thing. Except maybe the speed of your pacing.*

He couldn't tell which was more maddening: being trapped, or having Robin become the voice of his conscience, using the same tone as when she grumbled about marksmanship lessons.

Thinking of her reminded him that she and Esteban were still out there. If he had anything to be grateful for in that moment, it was that they should be well out of the way when Jack Knife and his band of brutes arrived in Glenwood.

Jaime, on the other hand…

Jack Knife, of all people. Using a map Wayne had drawn up.

He could not believe that Captain Dark Eagle's path ended here. The very notion was alien to him. It could not be that everything he'd been through—after Nowata, after Liberal, after Independence—that this cell was Captain Dark Eagle's ultimate destiny. No, someone like him could only go out in a blaze of glory, unbowed, never surrendering.

His pace quickened. His anger built. Soon, it would be all he had left. That, and madness. Sleep would be a long time coming, if it came at all.

An unknown time later, some faint sounds of disturbance filtered back to him. He halted, concentrating. Raised voices, though the acoustics in this basement made pinpointing their location impossible. Echoing through the ventilation system, most likely.

A *clang* resounded. Wayne recognized the sound, looked toward the door leading to the stairs. Sensing an opportunity, he shook free of all the distractions that had so monopolized his mind. His senses sharpened.

The door opened, and Colonel Edwards strode through, Major Oswald on his heels. Two guards trailed them, quicktiming it to catch up.

Edwards's thin face had gone a red so deep it verged on purple, a flush that had spread to his bald pate. A scowl twisted the features that had been so serene and smug several hours previous. He started speaking before he got even halfway to the cell: "What the hell is your game, Burleson? Talk!"

Wayne took a step back, confused. He'd expected just the guards. That Edwards had stooped to visiting the basement told Wayne that something had gone seriously wrong.

"I don't know what you're talking about, Colonel."

Edwards reached the cell, jabbed a finger in Wayne's direction. "Don't play that crap with me, Burleson, or by God, I'll have you gunned down where you stand."

"Colonel, I swear don't know—"

Edwards turned to the guards. "Shoot him. Right now."

Silence fell. The guards goggled. They were both young and baby-faced. One of them bore acne scars on his chin.

"Are you deaf, or just insubordinate?" Edwards said. "I gave you an order. Or do I have to do everything around here myself?"

Wide-eyed, the guards fumbled for their weapons.

Oswald put a hand on Edwards's shoulder. "Colonel, I think he may be telling the truth."

Edwards shook it off. "Well, *I* think his entire story was a ruse to get inside."

"But to what end? They didn't need him here if the objective was to blow up the bridge. They could have done that just as easily with him on the other side of the river."

Wayne cocked his head, unsure he'd heard correctly. "Has something happened to the bridge?"

Edwards bared his teeth and reached through the bars, grabbing Wayne by the collar of his white jumpsuit before he could react. Edwards yanked, bringing Wayne's face to within inches of his own. "*Don't play that game with me! Do you know who I am?*"

Spittle flew in Wayne's eyes. He struggled, but the colonel's grip was iron, and the fabric of the jumpsuit tough. "I…I didn't—"

Edwards released him with a shove and turned away. Wayne stumbled backward, arms pinwheeling just enough for him to regain his balance. The guards remained rooted to their positions, glancing uncertainly from their CO to Wayne.

Oswald addressed them: "You two. Dismissed."

The acne-scarred guard said, "Ah…Colonel?"

His back to them, Edwards said, "You heard the major. Get the hell out of here."

The guards retreated, the acne-scarred one elbowing his way past his partner in his haste to reach the door first. They were gone in moments.

Wayne allowed himself a small measure of relief. Neither Edwards nor Oswald appeared to be carrying sidearms, though that would matter little if they became dissatisfied with his answers.

He marveled at the Jekyll-and-Hyde transformation in Edwards. Only hours earlier, he had been the model of smooth command. Now, he resembled nothing so much as a pouty two-year-old. Such displays of temper in front of subordinates were bad for morale.

Oswald, at least, had sense enough to realize it. He said, "Forty minutes ago, at 2235 hours, our bridge sentries spotted a dark truck on the span, close to the Iowa side. The driver had approached with the lights off—in fact, had *backed* onto the bridge, towing a trailer that made the vehicle very difficult to see. Our sentries might have missed it entirely, except the vehicle's dome light came on when someone got out from the passenger side and quickly unhooked the trailer. The sentries challenged him but got no response. They opened fire, but he hid behind the trailer itself. He must have jumped into the rear of the truck, because the vehicle sped off, leaving the trailer. The sentries approached with caution, but before they got there—"

"Oh, God," Wayne said. He went cold and numb with shock, his legs unsteady. "Was anyone hurt?"

"No. The trailer detonated before the sentries had covered more than twenty yards. Crude explosives of some kind—gasoline, fertilizer, maybe propane—but enough to cause a section of the bridge to collapse. It's impassable now."

Throughout Oswald's recitation, Edwards glared at Wayne, hunched slightly forward. He had regained some of his composure, but his red face and the tension in the set of his shoulders hinted that he stood poised on a hair-trigger. "And you expect us to believe that you know nothing of this? That the timing of your arrival was pure coincidence?"

"I had no idea, Colonel."

Edwards raised a finger. "Jack Knife tells us that Captain Dark Eagle had a truck and a black trailer. And hot-air balloons are powered by propane, are they not?"

Wayne swallowed, remained silent.

"So: coincidence, Burleson?"

No, it couldn't have been coincidence.

Serena's people knew where they'd caught Jaime, knew the location of the crippled truck and its trailer. The woman was certainly smart enough to spot another way to get what she wanted. A simple matter, really, for her to locate Robin and Esteban, and deliver the same ultimatum she'd given him: Jaime's release for their assistance.

Or had it been the other way around? Had Robin and Esteban gone into town and offered a deal?

It didn't matter; the end result was the same. Serena could provide the explosives and some spare tires for the truck. The rest would have been easy. A minimal expenditure of her own resources, resulting only in the loss of trailer that wasn't hers, anyway.

No, not coincidence at all.

"Colonel," he said, "Serena Katz is a very smart woman."

"Oh, I don't think so." From a back pocket, Edwards pulled a two-way radio—Wayne's—and held it through the bars. "You said she has the other one, yes? Call her."

Wayne took it gingerly, keeping as much distance as possible between him and Edwards. "What do you want me to say?"

"I want to hear her account of this. You'd better pray it backs yours. And one other piece of advice: if you try to slip her any intelligence on what you've seen today, I won't take it well."

"Noted, sir." Wayne hefted the radio. "You realize that the effective range of these things is—"

"Now, Burleson."

Wayne flicked it on, noted that it was still set to channel three, the channel he'd always used with his team. He cleared his throat. "Calling Serena Katz. Serena Katz, come in, please."

He waited a few moments, getting only a static hiss in response. He tried again: "Calling Serena—"

"Why, is that you, Captain? I thought I might hear from you soon." Even over the radio, amusement showed in her voice.

The signal was pretty clear, given the distance. The range could be boosted if she were up high—in her castle, for instance.

Edwards extended a hand in a *get on with it* gesture.

Wayne said, "What have you done, Serena?"

"I should think it's obvious: I did what I had to do to protect Glenwood. As you didn't seem very inclined to cooperate when we last spoke, I thought it would be best to explore other options. It turns out that the other members of your team are more practical than you, thank God. That young girl—Robin, is that her name?—is particularly shrewd. How you ever got her to sign on with your little band is quite beyond me."

"She believes in what we're doing. Or she used to, anyway." The words pained him. "Where's Jaime?"

"I'm as good as my word, Captain. He's been released, and the three of them have departed for parts unknown. It only cost them your little trailer. A bargain, if you ask me."

"I didn't. How do I know you're not lying to me, that the three of them aren't lying in a ditch somewhere, covered with lime?"

She laughed. "Oh, Captain, you do have a flair for the melodramatic, don't you?"

"Answer me."

"What proof can I give you? They're gone. If you want to verify their wellbeing, you should talk to them, not me. I gave Jaime his radio back. Maybe they're even listening, right now."

Wayne glanced at Edwards and Oswald. The colonel's face remained hard, but the flush had faded. Oswald gazed at the radio Wayne held, brow furrowed in concentration.

"I doubt that," Wayne said. "Serena, what could you possibly hope to gain by destroying the bridge? Beyond mere vandalism, that is."

"Don't be dense, Captain. They were planning to roll over that bridge and invade this town. That will be considerably more difficult now."

Edwards's eyes blazed. He moved forward, as if he meant to take the radio from Wayne and give Serena a piece of his mind, but settled back, saying nothing.

"There are other bridges, Serena," Wayne said. "You can't

destroy them all. You might have slowed them down, but you haven't stopped them. In fact, you've provoked them. This is an act of war. If they needed an excuse for armed invasion, they have it now." One look at the expression on Edwards's face was all the confirmation Wayne needed.

"They never needed an excuse," Serena said. "And if it's war they want, it's war they'll get. While they're busy taking the long way around, we'll be busy, too. We will fight them with everything we have. We will never surrender. If they have any sense at all, they'll look at the smoking ruins of the Plattsmouth bridge and reconsider."

Wayne hung his head. "You cannot win this fight, Serena."

"Your tactical assessment of the situation is noted, Captain. Is there anything else?"

Wayne looked to Edwards. The colonel, lips drawn in a grim line, shook his head once.

"Not unless you're willing to tell me the whereabouts of my team."

"I have no idea. They're out of the picture, as far as I'm concerned. So, for that matter, are you. Good luck, Captain. And good-bye."

Static flared on the channel, and she was gone.

Wayne thumbed the radio off and handed it back to Edwards. Most of the fury had drained from the man's face, replaced by narrow-eyed calculation. "So," he said. "It seems that whatever else you may be guilty of, Captain, plotting to destroy the bridge isn't among your offenses. I wish I could say the same for the other members of your team."

"They were under duress, Colonel."

"And were *you* under duress when you flew over Plattsmouth?"

Wayne wondered, briefly, if it might be worth his while to play that angle, see if he could win a reprieve. Even as the thought took shape in his mind, though, he discarded it. Edwards wasn't really looking to grant clemency.

"No. Serena Katz told me you were planning to invade."

"She talks like we're some damned enemy army."

Wayne sighed. "If you had seen what I've seen, Colonel, you wouldn't find it so far-fetched. I don't know where you flew in from, but here in the Midwest, we've been cut off from America for far too long. People start to lose hope." He glanced around. "From what I can see, you've established martial law here in Plattsmouth. Is that what you're planning to do in Glenwood, too?"

Oswald said, "We don't use that term. But don't confuse an interim solution with the larger vision of restoring this nation to greatness."

Wayne had heard that rationalization before. It sounded remarkably like the President's final address. "Is that what you're calling Jack Knife? An interim solution? Colonel, I find it hard to believe you can't see that man for what he is."

Edwards put up a hand. "Spare me your lectures. I have a job to do. It's not always a clean one. And you were right when you told the Katz woman that she can't win. If she thinks blowing up a bridge will give me pause, she's sorely mistaken. I think she's bluffing. I think she can't possibly have the resources to withstand us."

Wayne thought Edwards could very well be right. Glenwood couldn't win in a straight fight. But guerilla warfare and terrorist tactics could prolong the conflict for a while. Force of arms alone wouldn't avail Serena, but if she could hold out long enough, she could hope to break her enemy's will. And in the meantime, a lot of people on both sides would die.

Edwards drew himself up, stowed the radio in his back pocket. "That will be all, Captain. I have an attack to plan."

He headed for the exit door. Oswald lingered, his gaze meeting Wayne's.

Wayne knew in that moment that if he let Edwards leave, he would rot in this cell until the Battle of Glenwood was over—assuming he wasn't executed first.

"Colonel," Wayne said.

Edwards paused, turned back to him. "What now?"

"What if I told you there is another way to accomplish your mission in Glenwood? A way that wouldn't risk any of your men?"

Edwards's mouth quirked. He glanced at Oswald. "I'd say you were stalling. I'd say you were so desperate to save your skin that you'd promise anything. Then I'd say you are in no position to negotiate with me, and that you should know better by now. All right? We done?"

Without waiting for an answer, Edwards turned on his heel and walked away.

Wayne called after him: "Don't let it happen like this, Colonel! Prove Serena wrong! At least listen to what I—"

The door to the stairs slammed shut behind Edwards.

Major Oswald, however, remained.

He stepped slowly back to the cell. He adjusted his glasses with one hand, regarding Wayne with a bland, unreadable expression.

Wayne didn't know what to make of the man. "And what would *you* say, Major?"

"The colonel is a smart man. He doesn't like being crossed, that's for sure. But he's shrewd enough to recognize a loose cannon when he sees one. You've given him no good reason to trust you. Of course he's going to walk away."

"But you're still here."

"Maybe I like to keep my options open."

"And you'd be willing to trust a loose cannon like me?"

"That depends on what you ask me to do." He unbuttoned his right shirt sleeve, rolled it up, exposing his bare forearm. It bore a Second Battalion tattoo, a twin of the one on Wayne's shoulder.

Wayne stared at it for long moments. Hope rose in him. "It would be an awful lot. Probably more than you'd be willing to risk your CO finding out about."

Oswald rolled his sleeve down and rebuttoned it, shaking his head as he did so. "The colonel is smart enough to keep his options open, too. You're familiar with the concept of implied orders, aren't you, Burleson?"

Wayne rose on the balls of his feet, stretching his joints. "Yes, sir, I am. I've even heard of plausible deniability."

"Good. So tell me your plan."

Wayne looked over his shoulder at the cot behind him. "Do you mind if I sit while we talk?"

CHAPTER SEVEN

THE LIBERATION OF GLENWOOD

An hour before dawn, Wayne rode alone down County Road H40 in some stranger's Chevy pickup truck. It had to be at least twenty years old, judging from the scabrous rust spreading from the wheel wells and the undercarriage. The manual transmission fought him when he switched gears. The upholstery—torn, grimy, and sprung—probably hadn't been much to look at even when it was new. Dirt and mud streaked the body; the windshield bore a long, winding crack. An old farm truck, Wayne figured.

He used only the driving lights, and those only because he was too unfamiliar with the roads around here. He would have preferred no lights at all, but the dark was still too deep for that.

He kept glancing in his rear-view mirror, though he had no real fear of being pursued. Oswald had skillfully arranged his "escape"—which involved sneaking him out of his cell and getting him outside unseen, where the old Chevy had been waiting, its bed already loaded with the supplies Wayne had specified. Oswald had driven the truck himself, with Wayne crouched out of sight on the passenger side, until they left the darkened streets of Plattsmouth behind and reached the sentry point south of town. The two grunts manning the post knew better than to question an officer's orders to forget they'd ever seen the pickup. Wayne wondered if Oswald had a bit of intelligence training in his repertoire.

Even so, the whole cloak-and-dagger routine didn't preclude the major having him surreptitiously followed. Quite the opposite, actually. Oswald—and his boss—had a vested interest in making sure Wayne held up his end of the bargain. So Wayne kept checking his six.

The drive southward to the Nebraska City bridge, over pocked and partially blocked roads, had taken nearly an hour, twice as long as it should have. The return northbound on I-29 had been easier going, at least, but he was decidedly behind schedule now, with a lot of work ahead of him.

"Are you sure you can do this alone?" Oswald had said as the truck approached the sentry post.

"It will be difficult," Wayne had said. "Time consuming, too. But not impossible."

"Whatever you say." Oswald looked him up and down. He had acquired Wayne's clothing, backpack, and even his weapons. Even in the dead of night, with most of the town fast asleep, the white jumpsuit would have attracted attention. "Make this work, and there will be no need for us to move into Glenwood. You have my word, Burleson—Captain."

He had stuck out his hand. Wayne had hesitated before taking it.

He'd felt fairly confident when speaking with Oswald. Now, alone in dark, hostile country, his certainty wavered. The events of the past several days had been enough to shake his faith in much that he had once clung to, even as his world had disintegrated around him.

America has fallen. There is *no America anymore.*

That had been Serena. Much as Wayne hated admitting it, she'd had a point…assuming Edwards represented the best America had left to offer. The bargain with Oswald made Wayne feel soiled, but it was the only way he could get out of that jail cell and back into the field, where he could make a difference. If it worked, he would avert this impending war, save a number of lives on both sides of the river.

I've begun to think that all this…this grand plan of yours is just some expression of your vanity.

Robin's voice, back again after a long silence, filling him with yet more doubt.

"No," he said under his breath.

The truck's odometer still worked, praise God. He knew roughly how far he'd walked down this road only twenty-four hours ago—no more than two miles. He'd driven about that distance. No readily identifiable landmarks presented themselves, but it didn't matter. He was in the vicinity. He turned off the road, going cross-country, headed north.

The truck's suspension took a beating, as did Wayne. His grip on the steering wheel was all that kept him from banging his head on the roof of the cab. He had no choice but to turn on the headlights; the way forward was simply too treacherous. A single wrong decision could drop the truck into a deep ditch or break an axle. He'd be fortunate to reach his destination with all four tires still holding air. He consoled himself with the knowledge that it wouldn't take long.

The rough ride was good for one thing, at least: it knocked all his doubts and fears from the forefront of his mind. He had no time for them, anyway. The growing light in the eastern sky gnawed at his peripheral vision, inciting an urge to hurry that could well prove disastrous.

He had a frightening moment on the downslope of a grassy hill, when one of the front wheels hit a patch of either gravel or slippery mud. The truck slid sideways, threatening to tip—or worse yet, to roll. He took his foot off the gas and turned the wheel hard. The truck shuddered and the tires bit once again. Wayne regained control, straightened his course, and reached the bottom of the hill safely.

The near miss left him panting, his palms slicked with sweat. He berated himself for his foolishness in trying to maneuver a rickety old farm truck like it was a jeep. A measure, perhaps, of how rattled and distracted he was. If he didn't start paying closer attention to the task at hand, he would doom the mission to failure.

"Pull yourself together, Burleson," he whispered. "One last time, that's all."

That had been part of the agreement with Oswald. "We can't have you flying around at will, stirring up trouble," the major had said. "Those days are past. After this mission, that balloon is permanently grounded, understand?"

Wayne hadn't thought that Captain Dark Eagle's final flight

would come so soon. And what would become of him afterward? How would he make his way in the world?

There. He was second-guessing himself again. A deal was a deal. He didn't have to like it; lives literally depended on it, and that was enough.

"Foolish old man. Pull it together. One last time. One last—"

The headlights picked out movement about fifty yards ahead of him, near a stand of trees. A deer, most likely…but no, too tall. It was a man in dark clothing, standing still before the advancing truck, legs apart, sighting down the barrel of a rifle.

Wayne hit the brakes, brought the truck to a skidding stop.

A sentry, out in the middle of nowhere, well away from town. It didn't make sense. Serena couldn't possibly have so many soldiers that she could afford to patrol empty, abandoned farmland. Even if she did, it would be smarter to deploy them closer to the city, so that they wouldn't have so wide a perimeter to defend.

The man walked forward, still sighting along the barrel. Wayne kept his hands on the wheel, but his thoughts were of the pistol tucked into his belt. With the headlights in his face, the approaching gunman would be effectively blind. Wayne could probably draw his sidearm and fire before the sentry got wise.

Whoever he was, this man couldn't be out here on his own. Wayne looked left and right for signs of a flank attack. The brush and trees to either side were dark and still.

The gunman shifted to Wayne's left, getting out of the worst of the headlights' glare and coming up on the truck's driver side. Smart of him.

Only when the man got within twenty yards did Wayne spot something familiar in his walk, and in his clothing. Wayne unrolled the window halfway, letting in the frigid early morning air. He leaned out and said, "Jaime?"

The man stopped. The rifle barrel dipped for a moment, then rose again. "Who goes there?"

Wayne couldn't help smiling. The boy was appropriately cautious. He'd learned well.

"It's me, Jaime. It's Wayne."

Jaime let the rifle drop. "Wayne? *Wayne*?" He ran for the truck.

Wayne got out. The two embraced moments later—carefully, both of them mindful of the rifle.

They stepped back and surveyed each other. Jaime appeared healthy. His eyes shone and his youthful face bore no new scars, though he seemed a little thinner since Wayne had seen him last.

"Jaime, thank God. Thank God you're safe."

"It's great to see you, Wayne. I knew you'd come."

"I thought you would be long gone by now."

Jaime shook his head. "I wouldn't let them leave without you. I knew you'd come."

"Them? Who—"

Rustling grass on his left cut him off. He glanced in that direction. Robin and Esteban emerged from cover, weapons lowered. Wayne tensed as they neared.

Esteban only nodded at Wayne, a mere acknowledgment of his presence. His features were stony as ever. Robin brushed leaves and grass from her clothes, studiously avoiding Wayne's eyes.

"Hello," he said.

Robin left off brushing, sucked in breath, staring at the ground. "Hello, Wayne."

"It's good to see you." Though he meant it, more deeply than he'd thought possible, he kept his voice neutral.

"Yeah." She finally looked at him. "We did what we had to do to get Jaime back."

"All right."

"So we don't want to hear any your crap about not negotiating with—what did you say?"

"I said, it's all right. It's done, and Jaime's safe. No point in dwelling on the matter." Given his own actions of late, he had no business lecturing anyone.

Robin's mouth bobbed; she glanced uncertainly to Esteban. "I...well, fine. Good. But you need to understand a few things, Wayne. Things are different now. We're not going back to the way it was before. We're—"

"Where did you get this truck?" Esteban said. He peered into the bed, though the gloom hid most of the equipment there. "And what are you carrying? Are those...propane tanks? And what is in these?" He indicated the white cartons stamped with a biohazard symbol and the words *Property of the United States Government*.

"A delivery for Glenwood," Wayne said.

As one, they looked at him, then at the cartons. Jaime took a step backward.

Wayne briefly recapped his exploits of the previous day. It already seemed so long ago.

"You went to *Plattsmouth*?" Robin's disbelief was plain in her voice.

"What did you think I was doing all this time? Sulking in the woods?"

"I wouldn't have thought in a million years you would do *that*. You believe you can trust those soldiers any more than you can trust Serena Katz?"

Wayne hesitated before answering, weighing his words. He opened a hand toward the truck. "They let me out of that jail cell and gave me all of this." He debated whether he should say anything more, but he knew he couldn't keep it from them any longer. They deserved to know. "But anyone who's willing to hire out Jack Knife and his band of butchers—no, I don't suppose I can entirely trust people like that."

Silence fell among them. Wayne looked at each one in turn, gauging reactions. Esteban was stoic as always. Robin eyes went big. Jaime's forehead creased. "Jack Knife?" he said. "Here?"

"Still looking for us. He saw me in Plattsmouth."

"Oh, my God." Robin's voice was small. She put a hand to her mouth.

Wayne let the news sink in for a few moments. Then he said, "Can you imagine what men like that would do to Glenwood? Especially if they were backed by a contingent of professional soldiers, fully trained and well equipped? There will be a bloodbath here, unless I can stop it." He considered. "Unless *we* can stop it."

Robin let her hand fall away from her face, swallowed hard. She looked to the brightening east. "You're losing the night."

"I don't want the night. This isn't a reconnaissance flight. I want them to see me. I'd hoped to launch at dawn. I thought I'd have to do it myself, which would take much longer. But with you three here to help—"

"Wait a minute," Robin said. "You *want* to be seen?"

"I'm counting on it, actually. That's the only way this will work."

"With Serena gearing up Glenwood for war—and you *want* them to see you coming? Wayne, that's suicide."

The thought had crossed his mind. "They won't open fire on Captain Dark Eagle."

"How can you say that, after what they did to Jaime?"

"No, he's right," Jaime said. "I'm not Captain Dark Eagle. I'm just some young punk nobody cares about. Captain Dark Eagle—he's something more."

Wayne smiled at him. Jaime had always understood, better than any of them. And even after what he'd been through, he still believed.

Wayne moved to stand shoulder to shoulder with Jaime. "That's the idea, anyway. Maybe they will gun me down. But I think this is the way it has to be. Knowing what's about to happen here—I can't just walk away. Captain Dark Eagle won't let me. What about the rest of you?"

He searched their faces. They all met his gaze, their expressions a mixture of uncertainty, apprehension, and grim resolution. The sight gratified him.

"Besides," he said, "if this is to be the final flight of the *Night Wind*, I don't think it should be under cover of darkness, do you?"

Esteban slowly nodded. "You are a crazy *pendejo*, Wayne Burleson. A little *too* crazy for me, sometimes. But I didn't come to this country just to let the bullies take whatever they want. That's why I joined up with you in the first place." He extended a hand to Wayne, who took it. They shook firmly.

"Esteban," Wayne said, "sometimes I think you're a better American than most Americans."

Esteban threw back his head and bellowed laughter. The force of it surprised Wayne. He'd never before heard Esteban laugh so loud.

To Jaime, Wayne said, "You know where the *Night Wind* is?"

Jaime pointed to the stand of trees that topped a nearby rise. "Right where you left it—just over there. Not that hard to find."

Wayne pulled open the truck's door and climbed in. "Let's get to it, then. I want to be airborne within the hour."

They set to work. He got the truck as close as he could to the trees, but the way proved a little too gravelly for him to gain the top of the hill. He parked on its shoulder, about twenty yards away, and the four of them went in to retrieve the envelope, basket, and burners. A quick inspection by flashlight revealed no visible damage.

They hauled it all to the truck and added it to the load already in the bed. Wayne and Jaime piled into the cab, while Robin and Esteban retrieved their own truck, hidden nearby. They headed back south, toward the county road, in search of a good launch site.

A bit nauseated by the rough ride, Wayne stopped as soon as the terrain leveled out a bit, in a shallow bowl clear of trees. He got out and left the launch prep to the others while he assessed the conditions. The sun would be up in another fifteen minutes, he reckoned, and the day would be clear. Winds at the surface were dead calm; he would need the *Night Wind*'s engine. A quick check of the battery showed it carried a fifty-two percent charge, ample for the day's mission.

As his crew unfolded and arranged the envelope, Wayne was struck by the strangeness of doing all of this with enough light in the sky to see by. They had become accustomed to and even proficient at operating in the dark, with only headlights, flashlights, and maybe the moon's illumination to guide them. By contrast, dawn was an ideal launch time for a hot-air balloon.

Wayne went to help Robin attach the collar, while Jaime and Esteban worked with the crown line at the far end of the envelope. As they worked, Robin said, "Wayne, I have to ask: is this mission just another part of your…whatever it is? Do you just want to go out in a blaze of glory?"

Wayne kept silent as he mulled the question. Prior to Plattsmouth, the very notion would have stung and offended him. He would have dismissed it out of hand. "I don't know," he said. "All the reasons I've given for doing this, they're good reasons, honest reasons. But sometimes I wonder if they're just…excuses." He double-checked a line connecting the collar to the basket, ensuring it was secure. "I'd like to think otherwise. But I guess an old man dressing up in a mask and flying into danger can't be considered entirely rational."

Robin stopped what she was doing, studied his face. He felt naked under her intense scrutiny.

"Wow," she said.

"What?"

"That's the most vulnerable I've ever seen you, Wayne. The most open."

"Don't get used to it."

She smiled, a rarity akin to rain in the desert. Even Esteban smiled more than she did. "No worries. But maybe…maybe it doesn't really matter why you do it, or why we help you."

"Maybe not. I hope you're wrong, though."

Dawn sunlight had touched the tops of the surrounding hills and trees by the time they were ready to go hot, though long shadows still lay over the depression. The basket lay on its side with the inflation fan positioned next it, pointed into the collar. Robin had to pull the starter handle on the fan several times before it buzzed into life. Someday, Wayne knew, he would have to repair or replace that unit—assuming he ever had need of it again after today.

He and Esteban held the collar open, allowing the cold morning air into the black envelope, which began to billow and swell. Some fifty yards away from them, Jaime stood holding the crown line. His job was to keep the balloon from bobbing crazily as it went hot.

They were ready. Without being told, Robin came over to take Wayne's place. He crouched by the burners, already lit, and fired them. Flames roared, and the air inside the envelope quickly heated. He squeezed the triggers every few seconds. The envelope rose majestically from the ground, fully filled out in a matter of minutes. The coldness of the surrounding air made the task that much easier. Jaime, still holding the crown line, slowly walked toward the basket, keeping the envelope steady. Robin and Esteban released the collar and, with Wayne, guided the basket upright.

Despite the risks they faced with a daytime launch, Wayne noted the excitement shining in Robin's and Esteban's eyes. His own face was no doubt similarly alight. Too often had they done this in the dark.

Wayne ran to the truck and removed the two large white cartons. Though bulky, they were light enough for him to carry unassisted. He set them in the basket, then climbed in himself. With the cargo aboard, he had a lot less room than he was used to, but still enough for him to maneuver.

He fired the burners again, while Robin and Esteban leaned on the basket to keep it in place as the *Night Wind* neared buoyancy.

Wayne motioned Jaime to bring the crown line in the rest of the way. The boy—no, young man—approached the basket and secured the line to a carabiner on one of the basket poles.

Wayne made a last adjustment to the propeller's position, clamped it into place, and surveyed his instruments. Everything was go.

"I'm ready. Untie me," he said to Robin, pointing to the rope that secured the *Night Wind* to the old pickup truck.

"Just a second," she said. She reached into a jeans pocket and produced the black mask of Captain Dark Eagle, held it out to him.

Wonder overtook him. He had been too preoccupied to even think about the mask. He'd lost track of it at some point. "Where did you find this?" he said.

"In the weeds by the basket," Robin said. "It must have fallen out of your pocket."

He smiled his gratitude, and tied it around his head. He stood tall in the basket. The balloon was right at the balance point; it strained against Esteban's and Jaime's combined weight like a living thing.

"It's time," Captain Dark Eagle said. Robin nodded and untied the anchor line.

"Good flight, Captain," Jaime said.

Captain Dark Eagle fired the burners, and the *Night Wind* left the earth. Twenty feet, fifty feet, a hundred feet, clearing the rim of the surrounding bowl and rising into the morning sun. Its warmth suffused him, such as it was this late in the season. He looked down to give his crew one last wave, then cast his gaze northward. He triggered the flames again. With one hand, he reached behind him and switched on the propeller. The *Night Wind* drifted toward Glenwood.

One thousand feet, and the city came into view, about four miles distant. His gaze wandered to the bluffs north of town, where the castle nestled. The trees hid it from view. He had hoped one day to set foot there, after it had been liberated. But that, if nothing else, had been mere vanity. The castle didn't matter. Let Serena Katz squirrel away up there; he had business in Glenwood itself.

Two thousand feet. Winds still dead calm. The land spread

below him. Though devastated by plague and social collapse, the patchwork quilt layout pattern that marked so much of America from the air was still evident. The roads down there were a mess, many of them devolved into bare ruts, but the outlines persisted, unmistakable. This sight, too, Captain Dark Eagle had seen far too seldom since his adventures had begun.

The propeller gave him an airspeed of eighteen knots. His course would take him to the center of town. He might need to make a minor correction or two as he neared, but that would be easy, given the luxury of navigating by daylight.

With the binoculars, he scouted the outskirts, alert for signs of sentry posts. The main access to Glenwood, U.S. Highway 34, ran just south of town. As expected, he spotted a roadblock there, consisting mainly of four old cars arranged in pairs, parked nose to nose. Serena had set up similar roadblocks to the east and south. She probably had another one to the north, beyond his line of sight.

Those were obvious defenses. She had no doubt made other preparations for the impending invasion, ones not apparent from the air. But the roadblocks were the line of resistance that most concerned Captain Dark Eagle. The sentries there would spot him first—if they hadn't already—and would call in an alert.

He thought again of his team. By now, they would be in the truck, working their way around Glenwood so that they could be in position north of town at the end of the mission. He trusted that they would evade the sentries—whose attention would be on him, anyway.

With another two miles to go, he adjusted the engine position. Just east of downtown was a small lake—a pond, really—that had probably once been the heart of a city park. It seemed the likeliest place for a landing. The envelope rustled and flapped with the course correction.

Satisfied, he opened the vent. The *Night Wind* cruised at 2500 feet; the time had come to descend.

With his attention divided among monitoring his instruments, guiding the balloon to the landing site, and watching for activity on the ground, he had plenty to keep him occupied—to say nothing of the fact that in another minute or two, he would be in firing range.

Through the binoculars, he spotted the first hint of movement. A knot of townspeople, running along what appeared from the air to be the main street, a north-south artery wider than the rest. They pointed directly at the balloon as they ran. He was still too high to hear any exclamations, but a faint noise filtered up to him, over the hiss of his burners—the slow rise and fall of a civil air defense siren.

"Good," he said under his breath. "Good. Wake everyone up."

The *Night Wind* dropped under two thousand feet. The siren brought more people out from their homes. Some stood and gaped, but most of them ran eastward, keeping pace with his progress. The binoculars showed him that many of the latter were armed with rifles.

No one seemed to be taking aim, though. Not yet, anyway.

"They won't shoot at the *Night Wind*," he whispered. "They wouldn't dream of it."

That had been the point all along—for the legend of Captain Dark Eagle to spread and grow. Unlike Edwards, these people wouldn't see him as a terrorist. They would know nothing of Serena's abortive dealings with him. They would know only that the legendary black balloon the ham radio operators had spoken of, the symbol of hope and freedom throughout the Midwest, had come to their little town. And they wouldn't fire.

Not even if Serena ordered it. He hoped.

Best to get the job done quickly, then, before she could mobilize and organize her people.

Under a thousand feet. He no longer needed the binoculars to see. Hundreds of people had taken to the streets of Glenwood and were converging on the park. He heard voices raised in excitement—or was it fear? The civil defense siren wailed on and on.

"Showtime," Captain Dark Eagle said.

He opened the vent again, increasing the rate of descent. This part of the drill he knew so well he could almost do it with his eyes closed. He killed the engine; the propeller slowed, stopped. He was less than half a mile from the park. In the absence of a breeze, the balloon's forward momentum would be enough to carry him where he wanted to go. A crowd already awaited him there, growing larger by the second.

Captain Dark Eagle waited until the last possible second to fire the *Night Wind's* burners. Some in the crowd below him cried out, perhaps fearful that he was about to crash, especially when the balloon didn't respond immediately. But he'd timed the lag perfectly; he reached a hundred feet before the rate of descent finally slowed, forty feet before it stopped, even rebounding a bit. He called down—"Look out below!"—before fall letting a tethered sandbag. Those directly under him moved out of the way, their faces upturned, wearing expressions of mingled fear and wonder.

He established a hover at thirty feet, over a grassy expanse at the southern end of the lake.

The land below sloped upward toward the west. Some low-lying structures that had probably once housed local businesses stood at the top of the hill, marking the edge of the park. The eastern sun bathed the area in glorious brilliance. He could well envision the children that had once played here, the young lovers who had walked hand in hand around the lake, the old men who had fished from its banks. He spread his arms wide, as if to encompass the entire assembly—men and women of all ages, dressed in ragged and worn bathrobes, sweatshirts, and blue jeans they'd had since the Red Death had first swept over the land, clothing worn threadbare but still barely serviceable—and said, "Good morning, my friends! Fear not, for the long night is over, and Captain Dark Eagle has arrived to deliver you!"

His voice boomed over them. They met his greeting not with wild cheers and bouquets, but with a low buzz and confused glances.

Well, life could be like that. Even the most theatrical of entrances could fall flat.

One voice rose above the throng: "I thought you only flew at night."

He spotted the owner of the voice—a young girl, early teens, long hair tied back in a ponytail, faded black shirt bearing the legend *Glenwood Rams.*

He smiled at her. "It is a new day, and freedom has come to you. I'm here to help you cast off the yoke of your oppressors."

From behind him, someone shouted, "What oppressors? No one's oppressing us."

Captain Dark Eagle turned. He wasn't sure who had spoken, but it didn't matter. "Oh, but you are, my friends. Captain Dark Eagle knows more about this situation than your beloved Serena Katz wants you to know. She—"

"Serena's good to us!" A woman's voice, to his left. She stepped forward, white-haired and rail thin, pointing an accusatory finger at him. "All she's doing is protecting this town! Don't you spread any lies about her!"

Shouts of assent rippled through the crowd. Captain Dark Eagle held out his hands, entreating them to be calm and listen, but his voice was lost in the din. Any moment now, he would lose complete control of the situation.

A new noise cut through the growing uproar—the bleat of a police siren. Captain Dark Eagle glanced around, trying to locate the source. To the north, the crowd parted, making way for a lumbering SUV that sported strobing red and blue flashers on top. The passenger side window was down. A rifle-toting man in sunglasses sat in the space, his legs still inside the vehicle, shouting orders. The crowd quieted as it neared.

"Let's go, let's go, clear the way," the man in the sunglasses said. "Clear the way, I said! Move!"

The SUV came to a stop at the edge of crowd. The man sitting in the passenger window looked up at the basket. "You! You're trespassing and creating a disturbance! Take that damned balloon and get the hell out of Glenwood, right now."

The assembly fell silent. Even the civil air defense siren had cut off. Captain Dark Eagle could hear distant birds chirping.

He said, "Sir, this park is public property. How can I possibly be trespassing?"

"No one is allowed in Glenwood without permission. So you just fly back to wherever you came from."

Another disturbance caught Captain Dark Eagle's peripheral vision. He looked to his left, up the hill. At the top of the rise, two more SUVs had parked, their occupants also wearing sunglasses and carrying rifles. They got out and stood waiting, holding their weapons in front of them, but not training them on him—yet.

He addressed the one who had spoken: "Where is Serena Katz? Couldn't she be bothered to come?"

The man in the window said, “On her way, don't worry. But she gave orders: you either leave, or we'll open fire.”

Captain Dark Eagle took a moment. He didn't need the time, really. He'd already assessed the tactical situation, could be summed up in a single word: *bad.* Not that he had expected any different. His course of action had been decided before he'd launched. He was Captain Dark Eagle; backing down from a tyrant had never been an option.

Every gaze in the crowd was now riveted on him. Expectation hung in the air as they waited to see what he would do.

So it came down to this—outflanked and outgunned, but still with one last job to do. Much better than languishing in an old jail cell or executed in some back alley like an animal. If this was to be the end of Captain Dark Eagle, he couldn't think of a much better way to go.

He cleared his throat, addressed the crowd: “I'd like to show you something. All of you. Something Serena Katz has been keeping from you. Take a good look, and if you still want to shoot me afterward, you go right ahead.”

He picked up one of the white cartons he'd loaded into basket, held it out over the crowd.

Instantly, Serena's men brought their weapons to bear and cocked them. “Drop it,” their leader said.

“Oh, I intend to. Do you have any idea what this is, sir?”

The man's sunglasses made his expression unreadable, but his gaze seemed focused not on Captain Dark Eagle, but on the carton. “Where did you get that?”

So he did know. Serena must have confided in him. Probably a second-in-command. To those directly below, Captain Dark Eagle said, “Catch this, will you? It's not heavy.”

“It's a bomb!” the second-in-command said. “Fire! Shoot him before—”

Captain Dark Eagle couldn't help himself; he laughed. “Nice try, sir. Very nice.” He sobered. “But you know better, and so does everyone else here, I think. I don't deal in bombs. I bring freedom. I'm Captain Dark Eagle.” He hesitated, looking from one gunman to the next, giving them the opportunity to fire. The barrels of their rifles wavered. One of them looked away, unable to meet his gaze.

And he let the box fall. Someone below caught it with a slight *oof*—the girl in the Glenwood Rams sweatshirt. "Hold on," he said. "There's one more." He picked up the second carton, dropped it over the other side of the basket. He wasn't worried if it hit the ground; its contents were well cushioned against impact. Nonetheless, another man rushed forward to catch it.

"Rather than bombs, what you'll find in those boxes are individual doses of a vaccine for the Red Death. Instructions are inside. Any doctors, nurses, or anyone with medical training among you should be able to administer them. There's enough for everyone in Glenwood, if the army's estimation of your population is correct. Make sure you store those boxes in a cool place, and try to administer all the doses within the next forty-eight hours."

"He's lying!" The second-in-command's face had flushed, evident even at a distance. "Put those down right now!" To the armed men at the top of the rise, he said, "Confiscate those."

Captain Dark Eagle looked down, addressed the two holding the cartons. "Do *not* let them get their hands on those, or you'll never get them back."

The second-in-command climbed out of the truck. The ones on the hill started down.

Captain Dark Eagle raised his voice: "If I'm lying, then what are they so afraid of? What doesn't Serena want you to see? What has she been hiding from you? She told you that Plattsmouth is planning to invade. Well, I've been to Plattsmouth. And now that you have the vaccine, the army has no reason to cross the river."

An angry buzz rose in the crowd. The ones holding the cartons backed away from Serena's advancing gunmen. A host of others stepped forward, interposing themselves. One of them said, very clearly, "I don't think so."

The gunmen stopped, cast an uncertain glance toward their leader. One of them said, "Gendron, what—"

The second-in-command—Gendron, apparently—extended a hand in an impatient, *what are you waiting for?* gesture. "Get those damned boxes!"

The crowd closed ranks. At least twenty people stood between the gunmen and the cartons. Some of them linked hands, forming a protective ring. The buzz escalated to a rumble.

Captain Dark Eagle smiled. "You see?" he said to Gendron.

"Now do you understand? No matter what's happened, this is still America, and we're still Americans. And that means *you don't get to choose for everyone else*. We have suffered, bled, and died for the right to decide for ourselves. Look around yourself, right now." He gestured to the protective ring. "Look at these people. They just stepped in front of armed men, put themselves in harm's way. And why? Because America isn't dead yet. It lives in all of them. You can gun me down if you like, but you can't shoot all of them. You don't have bullets enough."

The rumbled subsided, a wave of quiet spreading from the center outward. Gendron stood with his hands at his side, breathing hard, not replying.

It was a good speech, Captain Dark Eagle thought, and he had delivered it well. His only regret was that he hadn't been able to deliver it directly to Serena.

Strange that she wasn't at the park yet. If she had left the castle when the *Night Wind* had first been sighted, she should have arrived by now. Dark Eagle looked in that direction. With everyone else's attention riveted on him, he became the first to see it.

At the top of the bluffs nearest the castle, black smoke billowed.

Dark Eagle's radio crackled, and a faint voice issued from it: "Captain Dark Eagle."

Frowning, he pulled it from his hip and held it to his ear. His ground crew knew better than to break radio silence during a mission, except in the direst of emergencies.

"Captain Dark Eagle, come in."

It wasn't his crew. It was Serena. "Colonel Katz? This is Captain Dark Eagle."

"You bastard. You let them in. I hope you're happy."

The words came flat, inflectionless.

"Say again? I didn't copy that."

The radio went silent.

"Serena? Serena, come in."

A cry of alarm went up in the crowd. Others had noticed the black smoke, too.

Gendron pulled out a two-radio of his own and barked into it, demanding reports. The rest of Glenwood's rifle-toting militia looked uncertainly to each other. A few people started running, headed for the bluffs north of town.

"Dark Eagle."

A new voice came over the radio—stronger, masculine. He held it away from him, as if it had suddenly started giving off an odor.

"Dark Eagle, you hear me, motherfucker?"

The confusion and panic swelling around him faded, becoming unimportant. He stared at the radio, numbness spreading over him.

"Yeah, you can hear me. And you know who this is."

He knew. Though he had only heard the man's voice twice before, Captain Dark Eagle knew. It was Jack Knife.

"Just wanted to say thanks for providing the distraction, you son of a bitch. Made our job that much easier. Thanks for the map, too, man. Very handy."

His gaze stole toward the bluffs again, and the billowing black smoke.

"Want to guess where I am? We're at the castle. It's ours now." Jack Knife chuckled. "And I have a gun at that mouthy bitch's head."

Captain Dark Eagle mouthed the word *no*. Below him, the park was in an uproar.

"You know," Jack Knife said over the radio, "from where I sit, this Glenwood is a pretty little town. I think I'll like it here. What do you think?"

Dark Eagle looked around him. He and his balloon had been forgotten. Even the two cartons he had delivered had been cast aside. The attention of every soul in Glenwood focused on the smoke.

"Answer me, old man. Or I'll put this mouthy bitch down right now. I'll let you listen while I do it."

Captain Dark Eagle stood stiff, as if at attention, and brought the radio to his lips. "This is Captain Dark Eagle speaking."

Knife chuckled again. The sound made Dark Eagle clench the hand holding the radio. It was a wonder the device didn't shatter.

"All right, old man, listen up: you should get the hell away from Glenwood while you can. Because if you and I ever meet again, it's not gonna end well for you. But before you go, you have one last job to do."

"And what job is that?"

"Here, I'll let Oswald tell you."

"Major Oswald is with you?"

"Right here."

A moment later, the major's voice came over the line: "Burleson."

Dark Eagle's lip curled. Only at that moment did he realize how badly he'd been played. Colonel Edwards and Major Oswald had done for him even worse than Serena Katz had, something he would not have thought possible. He had allowed himself to be blinded by that blasted Second Battalion tattoo Oswald bore.

"You have betrayed me, Major," Dark Eagle said.

"When I want a lecture on ethics from a terrorist, Burleson, I'll ask for one. Now pay attention."

"I'm listening."

"Just so you understand the situation: we have occupied the castle. Serena Katz and her remaining personnel here are our prisoners."

Dark Eagle's gaze lighted on the two white cartons lying unheeded in the grass below. "And the vaccine?"

"You didn't seriously believe we would entrust *you* with something so critical to our mission here, did you? Those boxes are filled with toilet paper, and some rocks to give them weight."

The *Night Wind* was slowly losing altitude, but Dark Eagle didn't want to trigger a burn and miss anything Oswald said.

"The city of Glenwood is now under martial law. You, Burleson, will convey the situation to the townspeople. You will explain to them that anything less than full compliance with our orders will result in reprisals."

"And what are those orders?"

"The populace is to disarm immediately. Any of Ms. Katz's people still down there—"

"That's *Colonel* Katz, Major."

"—will surrender to us at the front gate at the castle. Once we are satisfied that the town is secure, we will bring in the vaccine and begin administering it.

"The prisoners will remain here, unharmed, for the duration of this occupation. But any attempted assault on the castle risks their lives.

"That is all, Burleson."

The *Night Wind* had sunk to a mere three meters. In moments, it would touch down. A few of the townspeople had remembered him and were looking in his direction—Gendron chief among them. He stood with hands on hips, waiting.

"Major," Captain Dark Eagle said, "thanks to you, these people will believe that I was part of this. They'll tear me to pieces."

"That's not my problem. Just make sure that you convey the message before you die. Consider it your final order, Ranger. Do you copy?"

Captain Dark Eagle switched off the radio and stood, head down, as the *Night Wind* hit the ground.

CHAPTER EIGHT

DARK EAGLE UNMASKED

He didn't see what happened to the balloon. They took him at gunpoint to the community center in the center of town. The building had once boasted a glass front, but most of the windows had long since been broken out and boarded up, and the one remaining pane featured a spider web of cracks in one corner. The interior was musty-smelling and mostly empty, but for a few long tables and chairs, and some piles of supplies—shovels, blankets, dry goods, and the like—along one wall.

The white cartons Captain Dark Eagle had delivered to Glenwood had been dumped there, too. As Oswald had said, they were filled with rocks and rolls of toilet paper. The latter, at least, would be useful.

As near as Dark Eagle could tell, Oswald had been honest about only one thing—the tanks of propane, five in all, one only half-full after the morning's flight. The major had no doubt counted it a small price to pay to allay Dark Eagle's suspicions.

Gendron and four of his rifle-toting comrades—two of them women, counter to Dark Eagle's initial assumptions—marched him into the building and sat him on a hard plastic chair in the center of the room. A large crowd gathered outside, but Gendron gave orders for them to stay out of the community center. "Once *I* know what's going on, I'll tell you everything," he had said to them at the time.

Gendron stood in front of him with his sunglasses removed and listened as Dark Eagle related Oswald's message. Serena's second-in-command was younger than he would have expected, with a thick head of curly blond hair, his boyish face beardless and free of scars. Dark Eagle put him in his late twenties.

Two of Gendron's people stood behind Dark Eagle. One of the women waited at Gendron's right. The fourth took a post at the door. All of them still held their rifles, though none had them pointed in Dark Eagle's direction.

Gendron took bad news much better than Edwards did, accepting the report impassively. That was something, at least.

When Captain Dark Eagle finished, Gendron said, "And you expect us to believe that you had nothing to do with any of this? That Edwards and Oswald duped you?"

Dark Eagle glanced left and right, but the mask limited his peripheral vision. No matter, he supposed. Mask or no mask, he would have to turn around to see what the two behind him were doing.

"I don't expect anything of you, young man," he said. "But if you know who I am, you know that Captain Dark Eagle is a liberator. I came here in the hope of preventing a war, but I was betrayed."

Gendron glanced at the militia woman to his right. "Well, from what we've heard of Captain Dark Eagle, he's not the type to let anyone get the better of him. But we managed to take your boy—Jaime, was it?—and Plattsmouth…well, we all know what Plattsmouth did. Seems like maybe you're slipping. Or maybe you're just not worth the hype."

"Or he's lying," the woman to Gendron's right said.

"Yeah, there's that, too," Gendron said.

Dark Eagle ignored the barbs and focused on gauging the tension in the room. Gendron and his team were angry, of course, as he was. But they could have easily thrown him to the growing crowd outside and had themselves an old-fashioned lynching. That they hadn't done so bespoke a certain measure of calmness, of rationality.

Or of uncertainty. Dark Eagle thought that much more likely, given Serena's imprisonment.

"Maybe I am slipping," he said. "Maybe I'm just a crazy old

man in a black mask. Or maybe I lied to you, and I've been working with Plattsmouth all along. What do you want me to say, young man? What proof can I offer you?" He looked Gendron in the eye, then shifted his gaze to the woman, then turned in his seat to look at the two behind him. Each of them averted their eyes.

He faced Gendron again. "I've already told you everything I can. Now it's up to you. If you think I'm lying, shoot me and have done with it. If you think I'm telling the truth, then perhaps I can offer you some counsel in this difficult time."

Gendron crossed his arms. "What counsel?"

"Strike."

"Say what?"

"Attack. Tonight. Don't give them time to fortify their position."

Someone behind him sniggered. "Yeah, right. They'll kill Serena and everyone else up there."

Dark Eagle kept his focus on Gendron. "Not if you strike fast and strike *hard*. They'll have to commit all their resources to defending the castle. They won't have enough manpower to worry about their prisoners."

The woman next to Gendron said, "How can you know how much manpower they have? Did Oswald tell you?"

"He's told all of us. With his actions."

The woman flapped a hand at him in disgust and turned away, muttering something about a crazy old man.

Gendron, however, took a step closer. "What do you mean?"

Captain Dark Eagle pointed northward. "How many soldiers do you think were on that plane? How many did they leave at Offutt Air Force Base? How many did they need to secure the towns between there and here? How many do they need to hold Plattsmouth? Edwards and Oswald are stretched too thin. They risk overextending themselves. That's why they've taken to using mercenaries like Jack Knife and his murdering bastards." As he said it aloud, he became even more certain. Serena must have suspected it, too—another reason for her to believe she could prevail against them. Too bad she hadn't shared her suspicions with him from the start. "At this moment, while you still have the firepower, you have them at their most vulnerable. This opportunity will not come again. Either attack now or surrender now."

Gendron glanced to the woman who had turned away. She shook her head. "I can't believe you're listening to this nutcase," she said. "You think he has any love for Serena, or for any of us? We're the ones who took his boy hostage."

He frowned at Captain Dark Eagle. "Yeah, that's true. If you're working for them, this could all be a setup for some trap."

"Again, if you think I'm lying, you should shoot me."

Silence descended on the room. The only sound came from outside, the swelling rumble of the gathering crowd.

His bravado collapsed with shocking suddenness. A deep sadness swept Captain Dark Eagle. That his beloved America had sunk so low. No wonder good people like Serena had given up. He'd been flying above it all for too long to see it, to feel it.

Perhaps even Robin had gotten it wrong. Perhaps delusions of grandeur had never entered into it. Maybe Captain Dark Eagle himself was simply a kind of denial, a retreat from the unpleasant reality his world had become.

It hadn't felt that way at the time, of course. At first, it had seemed like a sign from God—one that had taken the form of two figures walking up his driveway on a breezy spring day, the winds strong out of the south.

He'd been sitting on his porch and must have been dozing; they were less than a quarter mile distant. He should have spotted them well before then.

They had walked toward the house with no apparent urgency, much of a height, both humping backpacks. Wayne squinted, discerned a rifle or shotgun slung over the shoulder of the one on the left. Neither of them appeared to be carrying a weapon in their hands, nor did they seem aware of him yet. He glanced around, wary of a flanking maneuver, but the two seemed to be alone. Their clothing was filthy and ragged. Both had jet-black hair and dark complexions.

Wayne stood, wincing as he knees protested the motion. He held the rifle in both hands, barrel up, but not pointed in anyone's direction. Yet.

The two men stopped, exchanged glances.

Wayne walked to the edge of the porch. "This is my land. State your business."

The man on the left—the elder of the two, if the lines on his face were any indication—said something to his companion. The younger man—maybe still a teenager, by the look of him—nodded, raised a hand in a placating gesture. He took a step forward. "We're looking for work."

"Is that right?"

"Yes, sir, it is." His voice bore only the faintest hint of an Hispanic accent.

"There's no work here, I'm afraid. This isn't a farm."

The older man spoke to his friend again, his voice too low for Wayne to make out. The young one uttered some quick words over his shoulder, then faced Wayne again.

"Are you sure you don't have anything? We can do odd jobs—clear brush, patch holes in your roof, maybe. We can even hunt game for you, if you'd like some fresh meat."

Wayne glanced right and left again, alert for any movement in his peripheral vision. If an ambush were forthcoming, it would be at this moment.

But only the wind moved in the tall grasses around the house, and both men kept their hands where Wayne could see them, no sudden moves.

He allowed himself to relax a little, lowering his rifle. He could always drop, roll, and get into a firing position if he had to, and likely faster than these civilians would expect.

"My roof is fine, thanks. And I can hunt my own game. If it's work you're looking for, you might try heading down the highway toward Nowata." He pointed in that direction with the rifle barrel.

Both men shook their heads. The older one spat.

"You don't get out much, I guess," the young man said. "No way we could get into Nowata. Their sentries would shoot us on sight. Nobody gets in or out of there these days. That's a mean town."

At that, Kathleen's final instructions came unbidden to his mind. He'd obeyed her, as he always had, and in so doing had left her to a gang of punks and bullies. He could only hope and pray she'd expired before they'd gotten there.

Weakness hit him in the knees; he tottered for a moment but refused to let them buckle. Dad-blamed arthritis.

"Well, that's…that's a shame," he said. "A real shame."

The older man stepped forward, hands open. "Please, *señor*? We are low on water. Very thirsty."

He opened his mouth to inform them that the Verdigris River was only five miles distant, shorter than that if they went as the crow flies—but stopped himself. Kathleen wouldn't approve of him turning away thirsty travelers who clearly meant no harm, especially when the well provided more water than he could use. He even knew what she would say: *I was thirsty, and you gave Me something to drink; I was a stranger, and you invited Me in.*

He would not have it said that he didn't live his faith.

He said, "If you'll set your weapons down, you can come inside for a bit."

The young man heaved a sigh. "Thank you. Thank you so much. I'm Jaime. This is my father, Esteban." The two unslung their rifles and laid them on the driveway. They approached, the younger man smiling, eyes alight, the older one impassive, perhaps a little cautious.

Wayne set his rifle on the porch railing and stood aside, extending his hand to shake. "I'm Wayne Burleson. Come on in."

It occurred to him in that moment that although he'd raged at God a time or two, he hadn't spoken to another living soul since Kathleen. He supposed a spot of company wouldn't be a bad thing.

Wayne filled their water bottles from the well, and the three of them dined that evening on some canned corn and the last of his dried venison. It couldn't last forever, anyway, and as he'd told them, he was plenty capable of scaring up more. They spoke a little of conditions beyond the acreage, and the coming of spring. None of them volunteered information about their pasts, about the loved ones they'd lost, and Wayne found that completely proper.

After dinner, Wayne made a fire in the hearth, and the three of them sat around it, watching the flames flicker and dance while the wind outside gusted, strong enough at times to make the old house creak.

"So Nowata's closed off," Wayne said, crouching in front of the fireplace, shifting the burning logs with the poker.

"Yes, sir." Jaime drank from his water bottle. "We ran into a ham radio operator near Stillwater who told us that he'd gotten a distress call from there a few months ago. Said this gang had stormed the place, killed a bunch of people, and took a bunch of others hostage, to keep everyone else in line."

Jaime did most of the talking, occasionally translated for his father, and always respectful to his elders. Wayne liked him.

"They burned down the hospital, he told us. While there were still patients in it."

Wayne stiffened, laid the poker aside, looked back to Jaime. "The hospital?"

"Yeah. Scared of the Red Death, I guess. Can you believe that?"

Wayne set the poker with the rest of the fireplace implements, slowly stood, his knees paining him. He drew in a shaky breath. "Burned it down."

"Yes, sir. Real bastards in there."

Esteban said, "Everywhere, these days. More and more. Sad."

Wayne closed his eyes for a moment. The mental picture he got was too much to bear, so he opened them again, took his seat in the easy chair next to the fireplace. He sat bolt upright, staring into the fire.

"Mr. Burleson? Wayne?" Jaime peered intently at him. "You all right?"

"Yes, fine, thanks." The words came out in a monotone. "When did they do that? Right away, or did they wait a few days?"

"I—" Jaime cast a dubious glance at his father. "I really don't know."

"I see."

She had said she wouldn't last the night, that she might not even make it to sundown. For the first time, he prayed that she'd been right. The alternative—

"Somebody will take care of those guys," Jaime said. "Army, National Guard, somebody."

Wayne glanced toward the living room's north wall, where hung a framed display from his retirement party, including photos, a certificate of recognition, and his most prized ribbons and medals. It had been a present from Kathleen. In the firelight, he could barely make it out, but it seemed to speak to him.

He appreciated Jaime's sentiment but held out little hope of it actually happening. If there *was* an Army anymore—and Wayne clung to the belief that there was—the troops would have more pressing matters to deal with than trouble in some northern Oklahoma backwater town.

The hospital, burned down. With Kathleen inside.

A few weeks earlier, the very thought would have been enough to reduce him to sobs. But instead, anger constricted his chest, clenched his head like a band of steel. He rubbed his temples. "Nowata needs to take care of themselves," he said. "They need to cast out those bullies."

"Everyone is scared. The hostages—"

"Will never be safe. Not in the hands of those apes. A *hospital*, for the Lord's sake. They should have risen up right then and there."

Esteban and Jaime both cocked their heads at Wayne's words but said nothing.

"Nowata has given up. Like everyone else. They've forgotten that they're still Americans, and this is still America."

Jaime fidgeted. "Maybe. But they can't do it on their own. They need some help."

Wayne could not help it; he immediately visualized himself leading a charge on the Nowata barricades, raining fire on the enemy and bringing freedom to the poor, oppressed souls trapped there. He'd had such daydreams often as a young Ranger; so did most of the troops in his outfit. Everyone wanted to be the hero. As the years had passed, as the chances of fighting such a glorious battle receded, the fantasies had faded, until time and the approach of retirement turned them into ghosts.

But in that moment, they came back to him full force, with all the clarity and certainty of his youth, all the more powerful for the intervening decades, tempering his anger.

It was silly, out of the question. He was only one old man with arthritis. Even if Jaime and Esteban would be willing to join him, they were only two civilians, one of whom might not even be a citizen. Besides, Kathleen would never have stood for it.

Still, there had to be something he could do. With his scout training, he could at least provide some recon data, something that the people of Nowata could use to plan an attack.

Even that work would be risky, though, and he could hardly move as quickly as he would need to, given the state of his knees. Unless he scouted Nowata from the air…

Wayne's breathing slowed.

A new vision came to him: instead of storming the barricades, of flying over Nowata on a moonless night—invisible, silent, undetectable. He even had some night vision binoculars in storage; he used to stargaze with them when he went camping.

If he could only figure out a way to get the recon data to the people of Nowata, they would—

What? Take up arms against their oppressors at the exhortation of an old man? Of course they wouldn't. It would take something more impressive than that to motivate them.

God still has a plan for you.

Kathleen's words had seemed hollow at the time, but they resonated now, sonorous as a gong. His pulse quickened. In her final extremity, she'd seen something he'd been blind to.

Everyone wanted to be the hero, even in these debased times. And *that* was what Nowata needed, even more than recon data. Something transcendent, larger than life. Heroism. Inspiration. Hope.

Jaime and Esteban were looking at him, their expressions mirror images of expectation. Maybe they'd seen something in his face.

He'd pushed himself out of his easy chair, stood. "You boys are welcome to stay here for the night, if you'd like."

"We would," Jaime had said. "Thank you so much."

"I'm going to bed. Give the fire a poke every now and then." He had headed toward the stairs, paused, looked back. "You said you were looking for work?"

"Yes."

"Could be that I have some for you. We'll talk in the morning."

He'd gone up the stairs, and for the first time since Kathleen had gotten sick, he had not dreaded sleep.

But maybe he'd been kidding himself, even then. He no longer knew. With one hand, Captain Dark Eagle reached behind him and undid his mask, let it fall away from his face. Wayne Burleson faced his captors, his eyes stinging with repressed tears. Gendron reared back a little, as if Wayne had raised a hand to him. The one standing at the door gasped. The two standing behind him came around to see. Even the woman who had turned away looked.

"I'm not some superhero," Wayne said. "I'm an old man who's lost everything in the world he ever loved. But for all of that, I don't want to die. And even though I was misled and betrayed by Edwards and Oswald, I still share a measure of complicity in what's happened here. I want to help make it right."

"How?" Gendron said.

"Is the *Night Wind* still intact?"

"It's back where you left it. Why? What can you do with that balloon?"

Wayne sighed. "I'm not sure yet. But let me call in my team. Maybe we can think of something."

CHAPTER NINE

THE FINAL FLIGHT OF THE *NIGHT WIND*

Wayne rested against the truck and observed as his team worked silently through the launch drill. Cold drizzle collected on his brow. His joints ached.

Conditions were far from ideal. An overcast sky blocked all light from the moon. A front had swept in from the north, bringing a smattering of rain and occasional wind gusts. Though the *Night Wind* had gone unmolested, as Gendron has promised, the envelope had been trampled in all the chaos following the occupation of the castle, and bore a few tears as a result.

They had no time for such concerns. The *Night Wind* had to fly. On that point, they were all in agreement, even Robin.

They worked in the hills north of Glenwood, surrounded by tall trees. They'd loaded the basket and the balloon into the truck and hauled it from the park in Glenwood under cover of darkness, in case Jack Knife or Major Oswald had set up surveillance from the castle.

Gendron and his people should already be in position, but he had no way of knowing that for certain. Wayne had counseled them to absolute radio silence, with every move mapped out in advance. Two-way radio transmissions were too easy to intercept.

Wayne knew from his earlier reconnaissance flight that there were no trees within thirty yards of the castle. Gendron told him that had been Serena's doing; she'd ordered the grounds surrounding the castle cleared, to prevent an enemy from sneaking up on the place. Smart of her, but now it worked against them. Oswald would see them coming, thus negating any element of surprise, however meager. In an operation like this, every second mattered.

The key, then, would be to maximize whatever advantages they had. That included the *Night Wind.* For all its myriad limitations in battle, it gave the people of Glenwood one thing their enemies lacked—total air superiority.

Wayne watched the swaying tops of the trees, gauging the wind as best he could. It would make the launch difficult. An inflated balloon weighed some 7000 pounds. If a sudden breeze took it, the *Night Wind* would *move*, and they could do nothing to stop it. He could only hope the clearing they occupied was small enough and the trees tall enough to minimize wind effects.

Even after a successful liftoff, the conditions would make the flight itself tricky. The *Night Wind*'s engine would get a workout. At least Gendron had been able to arrange a recharge for the battery. But with so much of Wayne's attention focused on maneuvering the balloon, controlling not only altitude but direction, he would have no hands left for the rest.

That was where Robin came in.

It had been her idea, naturally.

"No," Wayne had said when she'd suggested it. "Absolutely not."

"Wayne, you can't—"

"No. It's too dangerous. You want to know why Captain Dark Eagle always works alone? That way, he risks no one's life but his own. Don't even think about—"

He stopped himself when he saw the way they all looked at him. Even he had to admit how silly those words sounded, after all that had happened. Captain Dark Eagle had been risking other people's lives since he'd first taken to the skies. Every liberation, successful or not, had its share of casualties. And not even the members of his team were safe anymore; Jaime's abduction was ample proof of that.

"You can't do this alone, Wayne," Robin said. "You'll need someone else in that basket with you." She gave one of her rare smiles. "Besides, I'm the lightest one here."

The others had concurred, and that had been the end of the discussion.

Wayne rubbed at his aching knees, then got back to work prepping the balloon for flight, before the team could accuse him of loafing.

The launch drill proceeded normally until the time came for cold inflation. At that point, at Wayne's direction, they set up two crown lines instead of one, manned by Jaime and Esteban, standing at the far edge of the clearing, about twenty meters apart. With any luck, the arrangement would mitigate some of the wind and keep the balloon under their control.

The *Night Wind* lay on its side, its black envelope stretched to its fullest extent. When Jaime and Esteban were ready, Wayne positioned the fan and started it. Robin held the collar open. The envelope rippled and began to swell.

Doubt seized Wayne then, a certainty that they had no business attempting this attack, that everyone involved would be much better off if they aborted right now, packed up all the equipment, and headed out, bound for parts unknown. One look at Robin, standing at the mouth of the balloon, businesslike and resolute, was enough to dispel the notion. That it had even so much as crossed his mind shamed him.

When the envelope was about half full, he shut off the fan and said to Robin: "I'm going hot."

She gave him a thumb's up, then passed the word to Jaime and Esteban. They acknowledged, barely visible in the darkness. Robin nodded back to Wayne.

He fired the burners, sending blast after blast into the envelope, and the battered *Night Wind* rose again. In minutes, the balloon strained at the lines keeping it tethered to Earth. The breeze caught hold and dragged the basket five feet, skewing the launch position. Jaime and Esteban dug in as best they could, which wasn't very well.

Robin shot a questioning glance over her shoulder at Wayne, while he kept an eye on the trees. The wind slackened for a few moments. "Get in," he said. "Hurry. This is as good as it will get."

She obeyed, clambering into the basket. Wayne signaled Jaime and Esteban to bring in the crown lines. As they approached, Wayne followed Robin. The basket, big enough to accommodate four under normal conditions, was claustrophobic with the extra propane tanks on board. The two of them had to stand hip-to-hip in the center. Robin came up to his chest.

Jaime and Esteban attached the crown lines to 'biners. The tops of the surrounding trees swayed again, presaging another gust. "Untie us," Wayne said to Esteban.

He quickly unhooked the last line, the one tied around the truck's rear bumper.

Jaime said, "Good flight, Cap—"

The rest was lost in another blast of flame. The *Night Wind* left the ground. Wayne hated to depart so unceremoniously, but they had to hurry.

Before they'd risen even thirty feet, a swirling wind wrenched them westward. Wayne fired the burners again, knowing it was useless. Before them loomed a great skeletal pine, long dead, its bare branches seeming to reach for them like giant hands. "Hang on!" he said to Robin. "We're going to hit!"

At the last second, the wind again relented, allowing them to rise. They almost made it…but the topmost branches snagged the basket. Some of them snapped off, others bent, but the last few formed a wall that brought them to a dead stop.

At least the envelope was clear. But Wayne had no time for subtlety or grace. "Shift your weight toward the rear," he said, and without waiting for her to obey, he leaned out of the basket and pushed the remaining branches out of the way. The basket tilted as he did so and might have spilled him if he hadn't succeeded. But the *Night Wind* came free and sailed out of the clearing and into the darkness, toward the castle.

The basket bobbed and swayed for a few seconds before stabilizing. Robin gaped at him, one hand clutching a handle. "Jesus!" she said.

"You know how I feel about that kind of talk, Robin." He got out his flashlight, quickly shone it around, ensuring they hadn't lost anything in the close encounter. Their gear appeared intact. He snapped off the light. "It felt worse than it actually was." Probably.

"That's a comfort."

"We're up. We should count ourselves lucky to have gotten this far."

"Yeah, lucky us."

He heard the tremor in her voice, belying her tough stance. He had to remember that she'd never ridden in a hot air balloon before; even under ideal conditions, it could take some getting used to.

"Look toward the horizon," he said. "That helps."

She nodded, her gaze riveted straight ahead.

Wayne checked his instruments. Already, they were a little off course, the wind carrying them too far westward. "I have to use the engine. Excuse me."

She shifted to let him past. He adjusted the propeller position and started the motor. After about a minute, the flapping of the envelope overhead told him that the *Night Wind* was changing course. The compass confirmed that they were now heading more or less in the right direction. Altitude, eight hundred feet and rising.

He fired another short burst of flame into the envelope. "I'll have to be alert for sudden cross winds and make adjustments on the fly. Be ready to move out of the way."

She nodded, still staring straight ahead. "Are we on course?"

"For the moment."

After a brief silence, she said, "I wish we could have said goodbye to Jaime and Esteban."

"Me, too."

There was nothing for it. Like Gendron's forces, his ground crew had been ordered to strict radio silence. Sentimentality at this point could get a lot of people killed.

He set a hand on her shoulder. "We'll see them again."

She swallowed hard enough for Wayne to see her throat working.

"How are you doing?" he said.

"A little better." She glanced skyward. "If it wasn't for the weather, this might actually be fun."

He smiled at that.

Robin dug in a pocket. "Here. While we have a moment." She handed him a piece of black cloth that he recognized as his mask. He opened his mouth to protest, to tell her that the time for silly costumes had passed…but stopped when she tied a similar mask around her own head.

"What—"

"Call me Blackbird."

"You don't—"

She raised a finger. "Don't argue. Just put it on." She gazed toward the horizon again.

He did as he was told.

The forested bluffs rolled out beneath them, silent and black. Robin—no, Blackbird—was looking down, a sign that she had at least gotten control of her fear. Captain Dark Eagle had never been prouder of her than at that moment.

At a thousand feet, the winds shifted again, becoming more northerly. Dark Eagle scrambled to readjust the propeller position before they got pushed too far off course. That done, he leveled off their ascent. They should be high enough, and he wanted to ride the favorable air current for as long he could.

The lights of the castle came into view, about a mile ahead. A fresh spatter of cold rain caught him in the eye; he wiped it away hurriedly.

Blackbird pointed toward the lights. "There."

"I see it. Get ready." He said a silent prayer for Gendron's people.

"Um…Captain? Aren't we going a little too fast?"

They were. According to his instruments, their speed was twenty-five miles per hour—a combination of a steady tailwind and the push from the propeller. They had to slow down if this operation were to have any chance of succeeding.

Dark Eagle grumbled and opened the vent line to drop their altitude a bit. The cross wind a little lower down would slow them. "I'll have to adjust the propeller again."

She shifted to allow him access.

"And light those," he said, nodding to the three extra propane tanks they'd loaded, a strip of oily cloth tied around the top of each.

"Now?"

"Now!" He spun the wing nuts holding the propeller in place and swung it back to its former position.

Blackbird got out the packet of stick matches from a drawstring pouch tied to her belt and bent over one of the tanks. She struck the first one. A flame flared, quickly snuffed by the wind. She muttered a curse and tried another match, using her body as a shield this time.

Propane tanks were tough to rupture. A drop from nearly a thousand feet should do the trick. But even that would likely not be enough to ignite the gas within—hence the oily rags, converting the tanks giant Molotov cocktails. The idea had been Esteban's, and none of the others had a better one.

Accuracy was an impossible dream. They could only hope to set off one or two of their homemade bombs inside the castle perimeter. If it worked, the explosions would be satisfyingly huge—and distracting. Oswald and Knife would literally not know what hit them.

If Blackbird could get the dad-blamed fuses lit.

The envelope flapped again. The *Night Wind*'s airspeed dropped to twenty miles per hour—still faster than Dark Eagle liked. Blackbird lit another match, cupped the flame with one shaking hand, and touched it to one of the rags. It sent out a wisp of smoke as it extinguished.

"Shit!"

They had less than half a mile to the castle. Dark Eagle was too busy minding their course to assist. Blackbird was on her own.

She struck a third match, touched it immediately to the rag. It bloomed into flame.

Dark Eagle's heart jogged. Fire in the basket was one a pilot's greatest fears. He reminded himself no refrain from any further burns for the moment.

"Light all three of them," he said.

She got out another match, lit it from the extant flame. "These tanks aren't going to blow up in our faces, are they?"

"No. Hurry!"

She lit the second tank, then the third using the same match. The flames from all three fuses whirled and twisted.

The lights of the castle glittered just ahead. Their window of opportunity had shrunk to mere seconds.

"Now, Blackbird!"

She squatted and lifted the first tank as she'd practiced earlier that evening, grunting with the effort. The tank went up and over the edge, disappearing from sight. The basket tilted alarmingly; the sudden weight change sent the balloon skyward.

Dark Eagle clung to a handle with one hand, pulled the vent line with the other. Blackbird braced herself against the basket frame, legs spread wide, and hoisted the second tank. As it went over the side, a *boom* sounded beneath them. Dark Eagle craned his neck to see a huge ball of fire rising from just outside the castle moat. A near miss, but one that should get Oswald's full attention.

It was also the signal for Gendron.

The balloon shot up again. Dark Eagle became queasy.

A second explosion below, this one right next to the large central tower. Dark Eagle smiled.

Blackbird hoisted the third tank…a little more clumsily than the first two. She fumbled it at the last second. It bounced against the rim of the basket before it fell away. The wicker there caught fire.

Before Dark Eagle could say anything, the balloon flew upward again. Robin spotted the fire; her eyes got big. She turned this way and that, frantically looking for something to use.

"Water bottle!" Dark Eagle said.

She groped for the nearest one, nestled in a pocket to her left, and upended it over the flames, quickly dousing them. Dark Eagle pulled on the vent line again. A fresh wind buffeted them, this one strong out of the south, a soft wall that slowed the *Night Wind* more effectively than any of his maneuvers had. The momentum shift staggered Blackbird; she grabbed the burner assembly to keep from falling out.

Activity erupted below. Several figures inside the castle compound had emerged to fight the fire. The *Night Wind* was still close enough for Captain Dark Eagle to hear their raised voices. Some of them pointed skyward. And from the east, where the only gate stood, came the first shots of Gendron's attacking forces.

The explosion from the third tank never came. Either the fuse had been snuffed in midair, or the tank hadn't ruptured on impact. A dud, then. Two bombs would have to be enough.

Dark Eagle had held the vent open for too long; the *Night Wind* started descending again. He released the vent line and triggered another burn to ensure they remained out of rifle range. The southerly wind slackened, and then the castle was behind them. Gunfire filled the night.

Dark Eagle allowed himself a moment's relief. The *Night Wind*'s part in the battle was done. The rest was up to Gendron. Once they got past the trees, he would look for a likely spot to land. Then they—

A bright streak in his peripheral vision drew his attention—a flash of fire headed straight for them, accompanied with a recognizable *whoosh*, a sound he hadn't heard in decades. A moment later, something detonated just overhead. Blackbird cried out and ducked. Dark Eagle looked up.

The *Night Wind*'s envelope was shredding, engulfed in flame.

Blackbird saw it, too. "What—"

"RPG," Dark Eagle said, his throat closing. Someone at the castle must have spotted them when he'd executed the burn. "Brace for impact."

The balloon fell out of the sky. Wind whistled past as the ground rushed to meet them. Captain Dark Eagle grabbed two nearby handles, bent his knees a little, shut his eyes, and started to pray.

So did Blackbird, after a fashion: "Oh God oh God oh God oh—"

The fall seemed to take much longer than it should have, as if time itself had slowed. The image of the *Night Wind*'s envelope in flaming tatters still played across his retinas. He had just long enough to think that it might be the last thing he would ever see in this life.

Impact, with a wooden crunch as tree branches snapped under them. The forest canopy would absorb some of the shock. Maybe they could—

And then the basket hit something unyielding—a larger branch, or perhaps the tree trunk—and they upended. Dark Eagle lost his grip and went flying. Numerous branches slapped and scratched him, tugging at his clothing, sending him tumbling. He hit the ground feet first. Pain exploded up his legs and the world went dark.

CHAPTER TEN

THE LEGEND OF CAPTAIN DARK EAGLE

Throbbing agony, light years beyond his arthritis on its worst days. His entire lower body screamed with it.

He shifted position slightly; the movement brought fresh aches and pains in his midsection.

So. Not dead yet, apparently. Captain Dark Eagle opened his eyes.

Dark forest surrounded him. He lay sprawled on his belly in a tangle of underbrush, the rich smell of earth and fallen leaves in his nostrils. With a long, low groan, he forced himself to turn over. His legs punished him for the motion, and a sharp pain stabbed at his side. He wound up on his back, his mask askew, looking up at the tree that had broken the fall—so to speak.

In the darkness, he could discern strange lumps hanging in the branches—debris from the balloon, he guessed. He saw no sign of the basket. It could conceivably still be stuck in the tree's upper reaches.

Nor could he see Blackbird. He opened his mouth to call her name, but the stabbing in his side wouldn't allow it. Broken ribs, to go along with his broken legs. That he could still feel pain, though, he took as a sign that his spinal cord had escaped injury. Small comfort.

The forest around him was silent, watchful. If the battle at the castle raged on, he was out of earshot. He had no way of knowing how much time had passed since being shot down; it could have been hours or minutes. Not that it mattered.

So the good Lord had spared his life, at least for the moment. But with two useless legs and other injuries too numerous to catalog, stranded and alone in the bluffs just north of Glenwood, he had to wonder how much longer he could possibly have. The night's chill settled into him, bringing with it a sense of finality.

The brush nearby rustled. Dark Eagle turned his head as far as it would allow. A shape emerged, a shadow among shadows, but with a familiar outline—a deer, either a doe or a young buck, judging by its size and lack of antlers. It stopped a few meters from him and stared, motionless. He stared back.

One of its ears flicked. Then it shifted its gaze, looking past him. A moment later, it turned and disappeared into the brush.

From the opposite direction came more rustling and the snapping of a twig, something that moved hurriedly, without regard for stealth. Laboriously, Dark Eagle turned his head to see what had frightened the deer.

Illumination bobbed among the trees—a flashlight. He could only watch as it neared. Calling out was not an option, even if his injuries would have allowed it.

The flashlight and its owner came on, lurching. The beam lighted on him, swung away…then swung back. Dark Eagle squinted against it, unable to raise a hand to shield his face. One arm was bent beneath him, and the other was still tangled in the underbrush.

The flashlight owner came upon him and stopped, looking down. The black shape was too large to be Blackbird.

Then he spoke: "Dark Eagle."

The voice was a man's, ragged but still distinct—Jack Knife.

Of course.

Dark Eagle forced himself to speak, though it pained him: "Evening, Jack."

Knife let the flashlight fall, the better to free his hands. He raised the rifle slung across his broad chest, aimed it at Dark Eagle, and sighted down the barrel.

From the ground, the flashlight cast strange shadows, lighting everything from below like some bad horror movie. Without the beam in his eyes, Dark Eagle could get a better look at Knife. Blood and soot streaked his face. One eye was swollen to a slit. His clothing hung from his frame in burned tatters. He smelled of ash and sour sweat.

Dark Eagle could not resist a chuckle. His ribs protested.

"Something funny?" Knife said.

"Just you, Jack. Are you really so frightened of a helpless old man with two broken legs? You always were a coward. Like most bullies."

Jack Knife's good eye blazed. "You want to shut that big mouth of yours, Dark Eagle."

"Why? You can only kill me once, you moron."

"And that's a damn shame. I owe you big time. First Independence, now this."

Dark Eagle thought to point out that Knife had beaten him in Independence but deemed it not worth the effort.

Something Knife had said earlier occurred to him in that moment, in spite of the pain and the creeping cold: *This Glenwood is a pretty little town. I think I'll like it here.*

Come to think of it, why *had* Jack Knife and his boys agreed to work for Edwards and Oswald? Why had he bothered to personally pursue Dark Eagle so far? Why would he want to stay in Glenwood?

Dark Eagle tried to speak but could only cough. Fresh agony ripped through him; he tasted blood in his mouth. He spat, tried again: "Did you lose Independence, Jack?"

Knife advanced a step, favoring his good leg. "You know damned well what happened to Independence. Those goddamned crazies from Liberal came pouring in and burned the courthouse down, and slaughtered most of my men."

"Liberal." Dark Eagle could only whisper it. Now *that* had been a liberation. How the good people there had heard of Independence's plight, he could only guess. The ham radio network, maybe. He supposed if Glenwood had heard of Captain Dark Eagle, word about Independence could have spread to Liberal.

Despite his deepening chill, a sense of peace filled him. He hazarded one last guess, judging from Knife's appearance: "And now you've lost Glenwood, too. That *is* a shame."

"Edwards will do for Glenwood, don't worry. And I'll do for you. But before you die, I want you to know that I'm gonna get back across the river, and I'm gonna lead the charge from Plattsmouth. Edwards won't try any more surgical strikes. Next time, we're gonna flatten this fucking place. And I'll make sure the people of Glenwood know that they have you to thank for it. They'll die cursing your name."

Dark Eagle smiled in spite of his injuries. He could have pointed out that if Edwards had been spread thin before, he would likely cower in Plattsmouth rather than risk another attack. But he didn't. Let Knife learn it for himself.

Knife stepped forward again, standing directly over Dark Eagle. The rifle barrel filled his vision. Knife said, "I'm sick of your smile, crazy old man. You die now."

Dark Eagle thought of his sweet Kathleen. After the liberation of Nowata, after he'd first made a name for himself, he'd gone to the site of the burnt-out hospital, and laid a bouquet of hand-picked wildflowers there. For the first time since the Red Death had taken her from him, the memory brought with it no pain. He would be with her soon.

A lone gunshot sounded in the forest.

A red spot appeared on Jack Knife's forehead. He jerked, arched his back, twisted…and fell, right next to Dark Eagle. The rifle dropped into the brush without discharging.

Overhead, a branch creaked. A moment later, a figure slid down the trunk of the tree and dropped with a grunt to terra firma, from about six feet up.

Even before the figure turned to him, he recognized the grunt, and the slight build—Robin.

Her mask was gone. Numerous contusions crisscrossed her face. A nasty gash marred her lower lip, but she appeared otherwise intact. Breathing hard, she stood with her pistol in one hand, trained on Knife's unmoving form.

She approached cautiously and waited several seconds before squatting and feeling at his neck for a pulse. She nodded once, then stood, looking to Dark Eagle. "He's gone."

He knew that, but he appreciated that she hadn't taken any stupid chances. "Nice shot. Especially for someone who never liked marksmanship lessons."

"It took me forever to get me into a firing position without him hearing me." She looked up. "I've been trying to climb down for the past hour. Not easy to do in the dark. And my head's killing me." She gingerly touched the back of her head with her free hand. "I'm a little dizzy. I might have a concussion." She glanced around. "Are there any more of them?"

"Don't think so."

She holstered her pistol and knelt next to him, gently removed his mask. "How bad are you hurt?"

"Pretty bad. Legs. Ribs. Some internal injuries."

She picked up Knife's flashlight, shone it on his legs, sucked in breath. A grimace pulled at her mouth. She quickly looked away.

"That bad, eh?" Wayne said. He'd suspected as much. His legs had taken the brunt of his fall. That fact had probably saved him from instant death, but he'd likely shattered all the bones below his hips. It certainly felt that way. "I think I'm done, Robin."

"You'll be fine," she said. "We have to get you—"

Raised voices rang out, close by. Robin stood, dropping the flashlight and whipping out her pistol again.

A host of bobbing lights converged on the tree—at least five, that Wayne could see. Their owners would have heard the gunshot, had probably seen the beam of Knife's flashlight. Within moments, they came upon Robin and him. She assumed a target shooter's wide stance, both hands on the pistol.

"Robin? Is that you?"

The voice came from Wayne's left—Jaime.

Robin relaxed, tilting her head back and closing her eyes, and lowered her gun. Jaime emerged from behind a tree, flashlight in hand, and embraced her.

The others came into view: Esteban, Gendron, a few other members of the Glenwood militia he recognized but whose names he did not know…and Serena Katz. Soot smeared her face, but she appeared unharmed.

She approached the tree and let her flashlight play over Jack Knife's corpse before turning her attention to Wayne.

"Captain?" she said.

Robin broke her embrace with Jaime and interposed herself between Serena and Wayne. "Step back."

"Look at him, girl. He needs help."

Robin pointed at him. "*You* look! He got that way saving your ass."

All around, voices raised in anger. The world wavered in and out for a moment. Wayne clung grimly to consciousness, though it hurt. If he allowed darkness to take him, he might not see the light again. Though the idea did not disturb him, he couldn't go out on this note. Not yet.

"Robin," he said, his voice no more than a whisper, lost in the din. He inhaled deeply, sending a fresh stab into his left lung, and called out: "Robin!"

They stopped arguing, turned to him.

"Don't…" He coughed again, bringing up fresh blood. He spat to clear his mouth, though the salt taste remained. "Don't blame Serena for this. I'm as much to blame as she is."

Serena stepped past Robin, knelt at his side. "Captain, we'll get you out of here, get you to the castle—"

Wayne shook his head slowly. "Don't bother. I'm finished."

"Don't talk like—"

"Enough, Colonel. What happened to Major Oswald?"

"Oswald? We've got him under guard at the castle."

"Good. When you contact Edwards—" He winced at a new wave of pain from his ruined legs. The blackness beckoned. "When you contact Edwards, offer to exchange Oswald for a shipment of the vaccine."

A small smile touched her face. "Are you condoning acts of terrorism now, Captain?"

Wayne would have laughed but for his pain. "Oswald is a military target. He's not a hostage; he's a prisoner of war. Treat him as such."

"I will." She raised her right hand. "We'll do it your way from now on. I swear it."

Wayne glanced at Jack Knife's body. "And you might want to contact Independence. Might…find some allies there."

She nodded. "Thank you for what you've done here."

"Let me talk…to my team."

Serena stood and backed away. At a signal from her, the rest of the Iowans retreated to give them some privacy.

Robin, Jaime, and Esteban crouched beside him. Jaime's eyes shone.

Wayne's breath came harder. Soon he would lose the fight to remain conscious. "Wish I had…some parting wisdom for all of you. Can't think of any." He glanced up, into the branches of the tree. "The *Night Wind* was good to us. But she's gone."

"We can rebuild it," Jaime said. "Glenwood will help. They owe us that much, at least."

"But who…will fly it? Even if I were to live, I would never walk right again. No…Captain Dark Eagle…is done for."

At that, Jaime, Esteban, and Robin all hung their heads, a moment of silent remembrance.

Robin laid a gentle hand on his shoulder. "Dark Eagle isn't a man. Dark Eagle's an idea. Soon to be a legend. Dark Eagle will live forever. And maybe…maybe Blackbird could find a book on flying hot air balloons."

With an effort, he freed his entangled hand, rested it on Robin's. "Maybe." His voice became a husk. "Maybe."

Esteban put a hand on his other shoulder. "*Vaya con Dios*, Wayne Burleson."

Jaime wiped at his eyes and turned away.

The world darkened again. The pain was fading, numbed by the cold. Wayne felt he might have been made of ice. Kathleen was waiting, and he thought she might be proud of him. "From Earth…I have arisen…"

Robin finished for him: "To Earth you have returned."

Wayne looked up once more, gazing into the forest canopy. Through the branches, he saw the stars.

The author gratefully acknowledges the assistance of Michael Jones in the creation of this work of fiction.

For exclusive content, freebies, and news from Matthew S. Rotundo, sign up for his newsletter at matthewsrotundo.com. Your email address will never be shared, and you can unsubscribe at any time.

Word of mouth is critical to any writer's success. If you enjoyed this book, please consider leaving a brief review wherever you purchased it.

For a sneak preview of *Apocalypse Pictures Presents*, another story about the Red Death, please turn the page.

EXCERPT

Apocalypse Pictures Presents

CHAPTER ONE

The scene wasn't working. He knew it, his leads knew it, and even the members of his ragtag crew exchanged knowing glances with each other between takes, no doubt believing him too preoccupied to notice. Had he not been so aggravated, Gil Thornton might have been grateful for the problem. Contending with a story issue certainly beat scratching out some means of survival after the Fall of Civilization. At least they weren't fleeing bands of roving marauders, or foraging for their next meal, or suffering from the horror of the Red Death, still lurking in the shadows, eager for a chance to kill what remained of humanity.

By comparison, figuring what was missing from the scene should have seemed like a day at the beach. But it wasn't.

They were shooting the Perfect Moment on what had once been a residential street in a small town that called itself Delano, some thirty miles north of the remains of Bakersfield. The Fall had spared much of Delano. Oh, most of its populace had still died, of course—the Red Death was an equal opportunity killer—but the ensuing riots, destruction, and social disintegration hadn't spread to this little pocket of the San Joaquin Valley. Better still, some of its infrastructure remained intact. Not much—a great deal of lumber, glass, and steel had been cannibalized, as it had everywhere, but houses still stood on this little stretch of road, and modest attempts had been made to keep the pavement from becoming too cracked and pitted. Old oak and cottonwood trees still stood in the afternoon sun, giving the neighborhood a lived-in look.

It was not the setting Gil had hoped for when he'd written the script, but then, nobody got what they wanted in these latter days. It would have to pass for a Queens neighborhood before the

Fall—so long as one squinted past the weed-choked, unkempt lawns and the scabrous rust on the three vehicles he'd scrounged up to make the place look a little less deserted. But there were ways to shoot around that. Gil had carefully set up the camera angles and blocking, and the rest would be fixed in postproduction. If their movie, *Better Days*, ever *got* to postproduction.

Except that the scene wasn't working.

Susan and Johnny ran through it again, slowly strolling down the street hand-in-hand, Gil keeping them in frame with his Sony F35 digital camera, sound man Terry Danson trailing them with a battery-powered boom mic, headphones covering his ears.

Susan Archer, dressed in a white top, denim shorts that Florence had expertly mended, and sandals, pointed. "Those are pretty flowers."

Johnny, playing Gardner, wearing a striped polo pilfered from some abandoned house they'd stumbled across two weeks previous, brushed aside a lock of long, straight hair that had fallen into his face. He had a knack for making such movements look unchoreographed. Though he stood a full head shorter than his costar, he carried himself with a quiet confidence that the camera just loved. The only one of them with any acting experience, Johnny Cascio knew how to use his dark good looks to full advantage.

He smiled a little, looking in the direction Susan had pointed. "Very nice."

Gil had written the dialogue deliberately dull. The words didn't matter. This was the Perfect Moment between Gardner and Kate, though neither one realized it at the time. To them, it was just a pleasant midday walk. Only much later in the script, after their relationship had crumbled along with the rest of civilization, would either one of them recognize the significance of this day. But for that climactic moment to work, the principals had to nail this scene, radiating happiness and hope with their body language, never explicitly acknowledging it.

They walked on, continuing to make small talk, with Gil tracking them. They hit their marks and remembered their lines—small surprise, given how many takes they'd already done. The camera functioned without glitches. The battery had been freshly recharged in the morning, so it had plenty of juice left. The wind was calm, so the boom mic would have no trouble recording the dialogue—which was essential, given that there were no studios left for looping. The sky was a clear, pale blue, the sun lighting the scene better than Gil had a right to hope, given the fog they'd awakened to. The day's shoot had everything going for it.

And still, the scene was…off.

Gil let it go on for another minute, hoping against hope that he would capture something salvageable. Finally, he said, "Cut," and powered down the camera.

Susan and Johnny glanced at him, weary resignation on their faces. Neither one bothered to protest.

"Any suggestions, boss?" Johnny said.

Gil set the camera gently on the pavement at his feet and stretched. "Let's take a break." He glanced around. "Who's got the water?"

Santiago Treviño, the crew's art director, gaffer, and grip, stepped forward, his laden tool belt clanking as he walked. He held a water bottle in each hand. Gil took one and thanked him. Susan took the other. Johnny walked in Florence's direction, no doubt to have her check his makeup. He was good about that.

Susan stepped closer to Gil. In a low voice, she said, "It's me, isn't it?"

Gil stopped drinking from his bottle in mid-swig and wiped his mouth. "Beg pardon?"

"It's OK. You can say it. I'm the reason the scene's not working, right?"

Gil studied her face, so intent and earnest. Actors. The technical aspects of filmmaking came so naturally to him—once one got past niggling details like securing enough supplies to stave off dehydration and starvation, getting permission to shoot in locations overseen by heavily armed and paranoid xenophobes, and working in conditions that could charitably be called primitive, all to make a movie that very few in the country even had the equipment to view. But none of Gil's skills with cameras, scripts, or lighting could help him deal with an amateur actress wrestling with her own insecurities.

The wrong word here could shatter her confidence, eliminate any chance of getting the shot. On the other hand, any equivocation would lose her respect.

Actors.

"Every actor loses focus now and then," he said. "We'll take a moment here, and you can—"

"Don't bullshit me, Gil. We've been working too hard on this for that." Her features hardened. "Say it, Gil. I think it's important for both of us."

He glanced past her. The rest of the cast and crew milled about, most of them staying near the line of two battered pickup trucks and one minivan parked on the other side of the street, the sides reinforced with plate steel riveted to the body, even partially covering the tires. The vehicles bore the legend *Apocalypse Pictures* scrawled in black spray paint across the steel plate. Their equipment, ammunition, and supplies were in those trucks, along with all the food stores. That made them the closest thing the production had to a craft services table, which was why most of the crew preferred sticking close to them. The others talked amongst themselves, occasionally glancing in his direction.

"Let me put it this way," he said. "It's not *just* you. It's—" He made a vague circular gesture with one hand. "It's a lot of things. Everything. It's a hard scene, maybe the hardest one in the whole script, and we have a lot working against us."

It had the virtue of being true, if not particularly helpful. This nondescript residential street was light years from his original vision for the scene. But when the opportunity to shoot here had presented itself, Gil knew he had to take advantage of it. Negotiating with "Mayor" Brooks, the balding fat man who controlled Delano and environs, had been unnerving. He was mayor in name only; elections had become great rarity in California, about as likely as the Aurora Borealis appearing in the skies over San Diego. Brooks had leered at Susan throughout their meeting, had even gone so far as offering to outfit and provision the entire crew if she'd be his girlfriend for the duration of their stay in town. Gil had managed to talk him out of that, offering instead a few weeks' work in the fields outside of town, payment in advance…and to make Delano famous for its role in getting the movie made—a naked appeal to Brooks's vanity that had seemed to work. Even so, the negotiations had left Gil upset, something he could not afford to let any member of the crew see. He'd been off his game ever since they'd set up filming in this neighborhood.

A lot working against them, as he'd said—but the hard truth of the matter became clearer with each successive take: the scene simply had no chemistry.

Johnny had the chops, no question. And Susan coupled some raw ability with a willingness to work hard. She had a particular problem with vulnerability, owing to her height and Amazonian physique; the denim shorts revealed startling definition in her quads and calves. But even when Susan was on, some essential connection with her costar was just missing. No one watching the scene could believe they were deeply in love with each other. Gil couldn't lay all that on Susan. Johnny Cascio, though a lovely fellow and a consummate pro throughout, had to take some of the blame.

Gil could see the problem, but not how to fix it. Recasting wasn't an option, and they had little time for a rewrite. Mayor Brooks had given them only three days' worth of his hospitality.

He could think of nothing else but to bull through the scene and get the hell out of Delano.

He opened his mouth to give Susan some empty reassurance, but another voice spoke before he could.

"We'll work it out," Johnny said. He stood at Gil's shoulder. His makeup looked freshly retouched. He offered a smile. "We always do, don't we?"

Susan grumbled and opened her water bottle. "I guess."

Johnny leaned closer to her, getting in her line of sight. "Hey, every production I've ever worked on had its share of crises."

"Yeah? Did you ever have to bring your own ammo to any of those other shoots?"

Johnny laughed. "Never even fired a gun until this one. But really, isn't it just a different set of crises? We'll work it out. We always do."

"I guess." She walked away, drinking as she did so.

Gil watched her leave, then turned to Johnny. "Thanks."

Johnny shrugged. "You don't have to thank me. Just telling it like it is. Seems like this picture is just meant to be." He nodded toward the trucks. "Think I have time for a snack before the next take?"

"Sure."

Johnny headed in that direction.

Santiago came over, tools clanking as he walked. "Hey. Mr. Thornton."

Gil inwardly braced himself. "Equipment trouble?"

Santiago shook his head. "No, no. No problems. For once."

Gil cracked a smile. Santiago rarely joked—not with him, anyway.

"I wanted to ask you something," Santiago said. "Where are they going?"

"What? Who?"

Santiago pointed to the set, the length of sidewalk Susan and Johnny had traversed ten times in pursuit of the Perfect Moment. "*Them.* They're out for a walk, right? So where are they going?"

The question startled Gil. Santiago had never before showed any interest in the particulars of the movie they were making. As near as Gil could tell, Santiago had joined Apocalypse Pictures for the work, a way of guaranteeing his next meal—inasmuch as meals could be guaranteed these days. He'd evinced little interest in the project itself, except in the most pragmatic ways.

Gil's hands fluttered as he searched for words. "Well… they're just…taking a walk. Enjoying the nice weather."

"Sure. But where are they going?"

Irritation flared in him. "It doesn't matter. They're just—" Gil stopped himself. Even as he said the words, he questioned them.

Santiago squinted, staring at the set. Gil had seen that expression from him before, whenever he was working something out in his head, like how to connect the sound equipment to a generator without fouling a shot.

Maybe it *did* matter, Gil thought. Maybe that had been the problem all along. Johnny and Susan were too busy trying to infuse inane dialogue with deeper meaning. They needed something else to focus on, a direction.

Santiago said, "Couldn't they be maybe walking to the store? Or going to the park? That would make more sense."

"No," Gil said absently.

Santiago shrugged. "All right. You're the boss."

"Not the park. Not the grocery store, either."

"Whatever you say." Santiago started walking away.

"They're walking to a friend's house. For dinner."

Santiago turned back. "They are?"

"Of course they are." Gil spoke slowly, wonderingly, as if just discovering the truth—or more properly, remembering a truth long forgotten. He shook himself. "You're absolutely right, Santiago. Thanks."

Santiago nodded. "OK. Good."

Gil pulled a set of folded pages from his back pocket—the day's shooting script. He patted his other pockets, searching for something to write with. Santiago pulled a battered pencil from his tool belt and handed it to him. Gil thanked him again and started scribbling. He scarcely noticed Santiago heading back to the truck.

Gil slashed through dead lines and replaced them with fresh dialogue. His excitement grew. No wonder there hadn't been any chemistry between his leads; they had been bored with the scene. As he wrote, he realized that *he'd* been bored with it, too. He could not guarantee that the new lines were any better, but his gut told him he'd finally found the right track.

Maybe Johnny was right. Maybe it was meant to be.

He was so focused that he didn't hear the SUV pull up, didn't notice as it stopped in the middle of the street some ten feet from him, remained oblivious as its occupants got out. Only the slam of the doors jarred him from his work.

Gil looked up. Mayor Brooks stood in front of him, beaming, sweat running down his round face.

Every time he saw the man, Gil couldn't help but marvel at his size. Obesity had become such a rarity since the Fall. He wondered if Brooks had been this big before the Red Death. Logic dictated that he'd probably been bigger. Gil found that hard to imagine.

He'd brought a couple of bodyguards with him, men in sunglasses, dressed in dirty, threadbare police uniforms and carrying shotguns. Gil had never had an interaction with the man without an armed escort present. The bodyguards hung back, lazing against the SUV, shotguns pointed at the ground.

"Mayor?" Gil said. "What brings you out here?"

Brooks glanced over the setup. "Wanted to check on your progress. See how things were going." His voice was a rich bass. "Doesn't look like much is happening. You folks finished?"

"We're just between takes."

"Hmmm." Brooks wiped sweat from his brow with one sleeve. "Might have a bit of a problem, then."

Gil cocked his head and stuffed the pages into his back pocket. "What do you mean?"

In an apologetic tone, Brooks said, "Turns out I had scheduled some road repair for this street today. I should have checked my calendar before agreeing to let you shoot. Sorry about that."

"But…can't you postpone?" He glanced around. "It's not like anyone else is using the road."

"We have an aggressive schedule. I want to get the whole town habitable again. Still a lot of refugees on the roads, you know. We have to turn people away all the time." Brooks shook his head slowly; his jowls swung. "Can't afford to fall behind."

Gil took a moment before replying. Brooks wasn't making sense. The street could use some patching, sure—but they could just as easily repair some other neighborhood today and come back tomorrow. And if they had some roadwork scheduled, they would likely have started much earlier in the day. Gil no longer owned a watch—he'd lost his last one years ago—but he'd gotten adept at judging the sun's position in the sky. It was well past noon, probably closer to two o'clock. Moreover, Gil saw no sign of workers with construction equipment, only Brooks and his two bodyguards.

Santiago and some of the others began drifting in their direction, no doubt curious.

Gil picked his words with care. "How long will the work take? We can be flexible."

"Hard to tell, I'm afraid."

"Mayor, I don't understand. Did we—"

Brooks held up a hand. "Look, I don't want to throw you off here. Tell you what: you keep working, but send one of your people back to my office. I'm sure we can come to some arrangement." He pointed. "How about her? She seems bright enough."

Gil followed the direction of Brooks's finger. He was pointing at Susan. She glanced at Gil, eyes widening.

Understanding dawned. Gil should have recognized the signs sooner. He'd certainly seen enough shakedowns in his day.

Gil's gaze flickered toward the bodyguards, still lazing against the SUV, holding their shotguns at their sides. The cast and crew held a decided numbers advantage, but their weapons were stowed, and they weren't in any position to cut and run. They'd had no reason to suspect trouble. Santiago took up a position on Gil's right; Gil felt better just having him there.

Maybe he could talk his way out of this. He crossed his arms. "Susan's on the call sheet today. We really need her here, I'm afraid. But if we need to renegotiate terms, I can offer another week in your fields." No one would enjoy that very much, but if it got this fat lecher out of their faces for the rest of the shoot…

Brooks clucked his tongue. "We have enough field workers for now. Best, I think, if you bring the girl over here."

From behind him, Johnny said, "Gil!"

Gil turned. Two more vehicles—a black Hummer and a rust-riddled El Camino, approached from the other end of the block, both carrying more of Brooks's men, all of them armed. Gil counted at least seven. His heart sank.

An ambush, then. Hardly the first one they'd encountered. Thanks to Susan's training, the team knew how to defend themselves. It had gotten them out of numerous scrapes in the past.

But this had to be the worst position they'd ever been caught in.

He turned back to Brooks. "Mayor, we're trying to make a movie."

Brooks folded his hands over his ample belly. "I don't give a shit about your movie. Give us the girl, and you can do whatever you want."

Gil looked over his shoulder at Susan. She stood near the trucks, probably out of earshot, and not really listening, anyway. Her gaze alternated between the hostiles at either end of the street. The Hummer and El Camino stopped next to each other, and their occupants disembarked, spreading out. Even at a distance, Gil could see the calculation in Susan's eyes.

The rest of the cast and crew drifted back toward the trucks. They knew what was coming. Good.

He and Santiago had the worst positions—in the open, too far from the weapons. Their gazes met, and Santiago gave a barely perceptible nod.

Further negotiation, Gil knew, would be pointless. But he had to keep Brooks's attention on him. "You know," he said, "it's actually a good thing you're here. I was just looking over the script and thinking that it's missing something. The scene's just not working. Isn't that right, Santiago?"

Santiago focused on Brooks. "Sure is, Mr. Thornton."

"What we need is someone with a commanding presence. Someone who'll make an impact just by showing up." Gil gestured toward the mayor. "Someone *authoritative.* You follow?"

Brooks's face crinkled. "Are you serious?"

"Absolutely. Mayor, ever since I started working on this picture, I've had to keep an eye out for talent. It's not like I can just put out a casting call in the trades anymore. I know ability when I see it." He manufactured a shit-eating grin, deliberately over the top. If Brooks thought him an obsequious buffoon, so much the better.

Brooks studied him for a moment, then burst into deep laughter that shook his great gut. "Kid, you are so completely full of—"

Santiago's right hand flashed out; he flung something at one of the guards leaning against the SUV. A big crescent wrench, which Santiago must surreptitiously have liberated from his tool belt, struck the man full in the face, shattering his sunglasses. The man dropped his weapon and grabbed for his nose; a gout of blood ran over his hands. The wrench clattered to the pavement.

"Get down!" That was Susan—an unnecessary instruction.

Gil hit the deck as shouts and gunfire erupted. He rolled toward Brooks, kicked at the fat man's knee. It buckled but he remained standing; Brooks roared and grabbed at the injured leg.

Behind Brooks, the remaining SUV bodyguard collapsed; he'd taken a flying hammer to the head, courtesy of Santiago's tool belt. Gil rolled toward him, grit and gravel stinging his eyes, and grabbed for the shotgun still clutched in the hands of the motionless bodyguard. Gil yanked it free but stayed down. Standing would only make him a target.

He scrabbled, turning himself around so he could see down the street. The goons at the far end concentrated their fire on the targets nearest them—quite smart, actually. A stray round in this direction might inadvertently take out their precious mayor. But it would also be their undoing.

Susan had already gained one of the trucks and retrieved one of the assault rifles—the M4 carbine, Gil thought—and knelt in the bed, just behind the cab, strafing the goons. Three or four had already fallen; the rest left off firing and scrambled for cover.

That gave the others a chance to pull out weapons of their own. They quickly took up position behind the line of trucks and blasted away. Rounds slammed into the El Camino and the Hummer, punching holes and shattering glass.

Santiago grappled with the bodyguard with the ruined nose. He had a screwdriver in one hand, holding it like a dagger, but the bodyguard, forced against the SUV, had a grip on Santiago's wrist. At their feet was the shotgun the bodyguard had dropped. Both of them kept stealing glances at it, their faces twisted, teeth gritted.

Gil swung his shotgun in that direction, hoping for a clear shot—but Brooks staggered toward him and swatted at the barrel, knocking it from Gil's hands. It skittered under the SUV.

Still bellowing, Brooks kicked him in the ribs—with his good leg, Gil assumed. Pain shot through his midsection; all the breath went out of him. He curled into a fetal ball.

Brooks stumbled for the SUV and yanked open the door, oblivious to his man and Santiago still struggling with each other. The SUV bounced comically as Brooks crawled from the passenger side to the driver's seat. A moment later, the engine roared into life.

The bodyguard looked over his shoulder, confusion plain on his face. Santiago got low and threw the man to his hands and knees, freeing his wrist in the process. Before the bodyguard could reach for the gun, Santiago drove the screwdriver into the back of his neck. The man squawked and went rigid. Blood from his shattered nose splashed on the pavement.

The SUV's tires spat gravel as Brooks spun it around and retreated. It turned a corner and was gone.

Santiago's man collapsed. The rank smell of shit reached Gil; the bodyguard had voided his bowels in his last extremity.

The goons at the far end of the street had clearly had enough, too. Those that could still run piled into what was left of the Hummer and El Camino; two more of them were cut down as they fled. The drivers wasted no time, putting the vehicles in reverse and fleeing backward down the street. One of the El Camino's tires had been hit; its tread fell off in chunks, leaving only a bare rim. Susan and the others kept pelting them. Both vehicles managed to get turned around and sped away, taking fire until they were out of range.

Quiet fell over the street, broken only by Gil's labored breathing. His ears rang with the last echoes of gunfire.

Santiago stood to one side, hands on knees, panting and pale, gaze fixed on the body of the man he'd killed with the screwdriver. A moment later, he doubled over and vomited.

Gingerly, Gil touched the spot Brooks had kicked. Near as he could tell, nothing in his midsection felt broken, though Susan would have to look at it.

His breath came a little more naturally. He forced himself to his knees, grimacing, then to his feet. "Santiago," he said.

Santiago pulled his gaze away from the corpse, wiped his mouth.

"We have to go," Gil said, wincing against the pain in his side. "Now."

Santiago nodded and straightened.

The others knew without being told. They were already gathering up the equipment and loading the trucks—all except Susan, who stood over a bloody, motionless form crumpled in the street, staring.

Gil opened his mouth to ask who'd been hit, but stopped when he recognized the striped polo shirt. It was Johnny Cascio.

If you'd like to read the rest, look for *Apocalypse Pictures Presents,* coming soon.

ABOUT THE AUTHOR

Matthew S. Rotundo is the author of the Prison World Revolt series. His short fiction has appeared in *Alembical 3*, *Orson Scott Card's Intergalactic Medicine Show*, and *Writers of the Future Volume XXV*. He is a 1998 graduate of the Odyssey Writing Workshop.

Matt lives in Nebraska.

Visit Matt's website at http://matthewsrotundo.com.

OTHER BOOKS BY MATTHEW S. ROTUNDO

Petra

Petra Released

Petra Rising

www.ingramcontent.com/pod-product-compliance
Lightning Source LLC
LaVergne TN
LVHW050556160826
845677LV00011B/2330